Fargo kicked the doo... men whirled, their faces suddenly frozen in disbelief and fear, staring at him.

"Having breakfast with a dead man bother you boys?" Fargo asked. One of the men, his jaw open in shock, twitched his hand toward his gun.

Fargo clicked back the hammer. "Don't even try. You can't kill a ghost." His steely eyes settled on Willie Drayton.

"You're dead, dammit . . . you're dead," Drayton hissed.

"That's right," Fargo said. "But I got lonely. Care to keep me company?"

Drayton snarled, pulling his gun and turning just as two shots slammed into his chest. For one long second, the rest of the men froze. Then, almost as one, they slapped leather and pulled out their killing irons.

Fargo muttered, "More the merrier," and opened fire. . . .

THE TRAILSMAN

AZTEC GOLD

by

Jon Sharpe

A SIGNET BOOK

SIGNET
Published by New American Library, a division of
Penguin Putnam Inc., 375 Hudson Street,
New York, New York 10014, U.S.A.
Penguin Books Ltd, 27 Wrights Lane,
London W8 5TZ, England
Penguin Books Australia Ltd,
Ringwood, Victoria, Australia
Penguin Books Canada Ltd, 10 Alcorn Avenue,
Toronto, Ontario, Canada M4V 3B2
Penguin Books (N.Z.) Ltd, 182–190 Wairau Road,
Auckland 10, New Zealand

Penguin Books Ltd, Registered Offices:
Harmondsworth, Middlesex, England

First published by Signet, an imprint of New American Library,
a division of Penguin Putnam Inc.

First Printing, January 2000
10 9 8 7 6 5 4 3 2 1

The historical material in this book describes incidents in the Spanish invasion of the Mexican peninsula, and the conflicts with the indigenous Indian peoples there. The facts depicted are drawn from records and accounts left by those who took part in the events.

Dates, names, places, interrelationships, descriptions of key battles, the scope of invasions into the mainland of North America, are all part of the historical record around which the rest of the story has been woven.

ACKNOWLEDGMENTS

Many thanks to all those who helped in researching the turbulent relationship between the Aztec peoples and the Spanish conquistadores, with a special nod to Ms. Marta Varela for her contribution on the Pyramids of Cholula.

The Trailsman

Beginnings . . . they bend the tree and they mark the man. Skye Fargo was born when he was eighteen. Terror was his midwife, vengeance his first cry. Killing spawned Skye Fargo, ruthless, cold-blooded murder. Out of the acrid smoke of gunpowder still hanging in the air, he rose, cried out a promise never forgotten.

The Trailsman they began to call him all across the West: searcher, scout, hunter, the man who could see where others only looked, his skills for hire but not his soul, the man who lived each day to the fullest, yet trailed each tomorrow. Skye Fargo, the Trailsman, and the seeker who could take the wildness of a land and the wanting of a woman and make them his own.

"The future is only the past again, entered through another gate."

—Sir Arthur Wing Pinero

1

Long before 1860, before the Trailsman rode the rich hills of the Colorado territory, the seeds were already sown.

Planted in the newly prized lands of the Americas, they were brought from distant Spain by those who called themselves the conquistadores—the Conquerors. These were seeds sown with arrogance and kept alive with cruelty and power, and they bore bitter fruit. The first of these conquistadores came in the early 1500s. Others followed quickly. They bore names steeped in their Spanish nobility: Cortes, Onate, Alvarez, Coronado, Olid, Cabrillo, and Sandoval.

The villages they ruthlessly conquered by force, trickery, and deceit were of individual tribes, but all members of the vast Indian culture in the land we now call Mexico, but the people called the "land of the feathered serpent" in honor of their main god, Quetzalcoatl. The Maya, the Inca, the Mixtec, the Toltec, and the most powerful, the Aztec, were their major cultural nations. Their societies were contradictory, combining the worship of religion with the worship of war, creating lofty architectural marvels while practicing human sacrifice atop them. But essentially, they were isolated people—simple, wide-eyed, welcoming, easily impressed.

And impressed they were when the Spaniards came in their mighty ships. One of the first of the conquistadores, Fernando Cortes, was quick to add this weapon of awe to his other mighty armaments, when his forces disembarked on shore. They landed arrayed in armor that gleamed in the sun, each soldier's head covered by a *chapel-de-fer*, or kettle hat, each proudly carrying their long, shining lances, their battle-axes, their gisarmes, glaives, and halberds. Even their horses, the huge, powerful Andalusian stallions bred from Moorish stock, were sheathed in metal, their heads cloaked with special armor called *chanfrons*, outfitted with eye flanges.

"See how they look at us," Cortes said to his captain. "They will be easy to conquer." His prediction was all too true and given further help by one of those strange confluences in history. According to Aztec beliefs, their great god Quetzalcoatl was to return at the same time Cortes landed on their shores. These strange and awesome beings were looked on as emissaries of their God. When Cortes came to learn this, he was quick to take advantage of the unexpected gift given him by the Aztec calendar, extracting eager submission by the far superior numbers of Indians. His every demand was met as being the will of Quetzalcoatl, conveyed by his messengers.

2

Cortes and other conquistadores were given gold, precious jewels, the labor they needed to build quarters, women for their soldiers, and all the food they could eat. In addition, the invaders hired thousands of the most primitive Indian tribesmen as mercenaries to act as foot soldiers wherever they met resistance. But as time went by, the conquistadores' demands became harsher, their actions more brutal, and the Aztecs began to think twice about the godliness of these newcomers to their lands. When the Spaniards, pressed by the bishops who had traveled with them, began to insist the Indians worship Christianity, violently punishing those who resisted, the fabric of submission began to tear apart. Uprisings against the invaders began to spread and turn into major rebellion.

But there were still Indian rulers who wavered in their attitudes toward the powerful invaders. One of these was the Aztec ruler, Montezuma the Second. Because of Montezuma's prestige and exalted position in his society, the Aztecs continued to bow to the conquerors, but it became an increasingly uneasy alliance. Perhaps it was only fitting that Fernando Cortes, foremost among the early conquistadores, was the main general at the beginning of the end.

The downfall took a good while longer but Cortes was there at that precise moment in time when the conquistadores gave rise to what they eventually called the *Noche Triste* . . . the Sad Night.

That moment began when Fernando Cortes marched toward the great Aztec city of Tenochtitlan.

Inside the sprawling city, a double hostage situation was taking place. Cortes had sent his aide General Alvarez to hold Montezuma hostage under the pretext of protecting him. But in turn, the Aztecs had taken Alvarez and his small force hostage inside the center of the city. As Cortes marched to end the strange siege, his lips twitched when he came in sight of the great city of Tenochtitlan. An island city, the Aztec capital was approached by great causeways that crossed the deep waters of Lake Texcoco. "I do not like this," Cortes muttered to his aide Navarez, who rode beside him. "There are thousands of Aztecs in that city."

"Armed with nothing to hurt our soldiers," the aide bragged. "Look at the army you command."

Cortes turned in his saddle to survey the force at his heels, his eyes moving over the thousand mercenary Tlaxcalan warriors, armed with spears but otherwise half naked, then the hundred and fifty armored horsemen and their fearsome weapons. It was indeed an awesome force, enough to impress anyone, yet Cortes could not stop the nervousness that curled inside him. "I would feel better if the Aztecs still welcomed us," he said.

"Montezuma is in the city in his palace. He still believes we were sent by his God. He will keep the others in line," Navarez said.

Cortes grimaced. "I wish I could count on that, but I can't. Many of Montezuma's people feel he has betrayed them. They no longer see him as their ruler, their leader. Worse, Montezuma does not know him-

4

self any longer where he stands, what he believes. He is consumed by indecision. A man that does not know himself cannot lead others." Cortes fell silent for a moment as he frowned at the causeway that stretched out before him. "But I must go on and free Alvarez. Anything less would certainly make us lose face in the eyes of the Aztecs. They would take it as a show of weakness, and we cannot have that. Pass the word. We march across the causeway."

Cortes sent his big black stallion forward and his army followed. With a slow, deliberate pace, he crossed the first of the flat, wooden bridges that spanned the gaps in the causeway. Knots of Aztecs appeared at the far end of the causeway, falling back as he neared. Cortes almost smiled. This was the reaction he wanted to see—the Aztecs shrinking back in fear before the spectacle of his army. As the Indians continued to recede, many vanishing into the stone openings of the buildings, Cortes neared the terraced steps of the Aztec capital. He glimpsed the Indians peering from the safety of the narrow streets that crisscrossed the city. The eerie silence continued to bother Cortes but he rode on, leading his army into the center of Tenochtitlan, with its acres of flat-roofed buildings, stone walls, and narrow passageways with only a few broad, open squares fit for an armed cavalry charge.

Suddenly, three Aztecs appeared carrying wooden clubs, wearing only ragged loincloths. They came toward Cortes and halted a dozen yards away. "Release General Alvarez and his men and we will spare your people," Cortes commanded. The three figures turned and walked away without answering, disappearing into one of the passages. But their answer came only seconds later. The conquistador's eyes grew wide as from every building, parapet, passage, and window, Indians appeared. They appeared on both sides of him and he saw there had to be thousands as they crowded into each other. Fernando Cortes suddenly knew one more thing. He and his army had been allowed to march into a trap.

He was still cursing under his breath when the very sky grew dark as thousands of rocks filled the air. Not thrown by hand, Cortes saw, the missiles were propelled by powerful slingshots that carried the force of a small cannonball. Reacting instantly, Cortes ordered his mercenary Tlaxcalan warriors to attack. They were his first line of assault, designed to absorb the enemy's first blows and entirely expendable. The Aztecs would quickly run out of rocks and men to fire them, and their wooden clubs and primitive axes were no match for the spears of the mercenaries. But Cortes quickly found out he had once again miscalculated. The Aztecs attacked with total abandon, flinging themselves at the mercenaries while the hail of rocks continued unabated. New attackers replaced those his warriors killed.

Seeing his Tlaxcalan warriors being decimated, Cortes charged his armored columns forward into the narrow streets of the city and the hoard of Aztec attackers. With the small cannons they call falconets, their windlass-driven crossbows, their halberds, gisarmes, broadswords, battle axes, and harquebuses—small-caliber matchlock long guns—the armored soldiers made the Aztecs pay a terrible price for their attack. Soon the stone streets of Tenochtitlan ran red with the blood of Aztec warriors. Yet, for all the carnage they created, Cortes's armored columns found more Aztec warriors attacking. "There's no end to them!" he spit out at his aide. "They are like bees swarming from a giant hive." He saw three of his men fall from their horses as their armor failed to protect them from a particularly furious rain of small boulders.

Cursing, Cortes drew his army back from the narrow streets and sent them charging across the open square to the palace at the center of the city. They quickly killed the few defenders there and swept into the inner compound, where he was greeted by General Alvarez and twenty-five of his men. Cortes dismounted and took stock of his army. He had lost over half of his Tlaxcalan mercenaries and some fifty of his main armored force. Twenty-five of those could be replaced by Alvarez's armored men. His force was weakened, but the core of it—his armored horsemen—were still formidable enough, Cortes decided. It was midday and the Aztec attackers had drawn back, their enemy protected by the walls of the inner city palace.

"I wanted to warn you but I couldn't," Alvarez said.

"No matter. We will fight our way out," Cortes replied.

Alvarez shook his head despondently. "There are too many of them. You saw that," he said.

"Not anymore. Their city is covered with Aztec corpses. They have learned what happens when they attack my army. Those left will not be so eager to sacrifice themselves," Cortes responded. "Where is Montezuma?"

"In the palace, under guard," Alvarez said.

"Leave him there for now. I will use him when they begin to weaken a little more," Cortes said and turned to his mercenaries. "Find tall pieces of wood and round strips we can use as rollers. We are going to build barricades that we can roll before us. If they still have thoughts of attacking, that will change their minds."

Under the supervision of twelve of Cortes's Spanish soldiers, the mercenaries found enough wood, twine, and round strips to construct four barricades. It was midafternoon when they finished and Cortes had his armored horsemen and Indian mercenaries move from the palace walls, pushing the barricades before them. It took only minutes before the Aztecs began to appear and Cortes frowned. They seemed to be everywhere, as many as there had been before. They attacked the moment the first barricade reached the edge of the open square, again filling the air with slingshot-driven rocks.

But the barricades, crude as they were, provided protection, bearing the brunt of the rocks that crashed against them. Cortes had the other barricades rolled up and sent his men forward behind them. But his brow darkened in disbelief as he saw the Aztec attackers leave their walled parapets and narrow streets to come streaming into the square. Ignoring cannon shot from the falconets, falling under the arrows of the great crossbows that sent their shafts clear through a human body, the Aztecs attacked in waves, stepping on the bodies of fallen comrades to rush forward with long poles. With suicidal abandon, they smashed the poles into the barricades. As wave after wave fell under the shots of the armored horsemen, others replaced them, driving the long poles forward to crash into the barricades again and again. Unable to believe his eyes, Cortes saw the barricades begin to splinter, then break apart.

The attackers, now climbing over small mountains of slain, bloodied bodies, continued their assault. All the while, the torrential hail of rocks continued to fall. Cortes tried to rally his men to keep moving forward, but the attackers were too many, their frenzied assault overwhelming. Finally, he ordered his men to fall back once again to the relative safety of the inner palace, General Alvarez at his side. Once inside the palace walls, Cortes again surveyed his losses. His mercenary warriors had been reduced to some two hundred and he had lost another fifty of his main soldiers.

He gazed out across the square and beyond to the narrow passages of the city. Bodies were strewn and piled everywhere, small mountains of torn and lifeless corpses. The superior weaponry of the Spaniards had taken a dreadful toll, leaving hardly a single

Aztec body intact. But the barricades lay in splinters and the Aztecs had drawn back to line the edges of the square, peering down from their parapets. "Is there no end to them?" Cortes heard Alvarez ask. "We have slaughtered thousands and yet there are still more."

"Bring Montezuma to me," Cortes ordered and Alvarez hurried into the heart of the palace. He returned moments later with six of his men walking beside the Aztec ruler. Montezuma wore his deep blue and yellow royal robes, Cortes noted. Deep creases lined his face, making him look older than he actually was.

"It is time for you to talk to your people," Cortes said. "Tell them to stop sacrificing themselves. Tell them we will not punish them for rising up against us. Tell them it will be as it once was between us."

"I fear they will neither listen to me nor believe me any longer," Montezuma said.

Cortes chose his words carefully. He had come to know the pride of ancestry that was a vital part of the Aztec culture. Each member of the family felt the need to equal, if not surpass, the rule of his predecessor. "Your father would make them believe. He would make them listen to him. Are you telling me that you cannot do that?" Cortes said cannily. He saw Montezuma's shoulders lift, his face take on the pride that the son of a great ruler should carry. "Make them listen to you and Montezuma the Second will be remembered as the greatest of all Aztec rulers," Cortes pressed.

Montezuma's body straightened and he moved

past Cortes, stepped out of the palace, and onto the broad square. Slowly, he walked toward the people who lined the edge of the square, his every movement commanding and deliberate. He reached the center of the square and halted, then lifted his arms skyward imperiously. Cortes listened to the Aztec ruler call to his people in a voice that held more strength than he expected to hear. He had learned enough of the Aztec tongue to understand a good part of Montezuma's words. "No more blood on our sacred ground . . . you have shown your bravery . . . They want to return to peace with us . . . Perhaps Quetzalcoatl sent them to test us . . . We have met the test."

Cortes was still listening when he heard the murmur from the crowd, a murmur that quickly became a rumble and then a chorus of angry calls. Suddenly a volley of rocks flew through the air. All of them smashed into Montezuma as he crumpled to the ground. He lay still as the shouts snapped off and silence engulfed the square once more. Cortes motioned to six of his men to accompany him, their shields upraised, as he strode to the still form of the Aztec ruler. He halted beside the blue and yellow robes that were now streaked with red as Montezuma bled from a crushed skull and a hole where one of his eyes had been.

Montezuma the Second was dead. Cortes and his men retreated backward into the palace. "It is over for us," Alvarez said. "I know it, the men know it. They are without heart now. They realize we cannot fight

11

our way out. Some want to surrender and ask for mercy."

"They'll get none," Cortes snapped. "But we are going to get out and I'll give the men something to lift their spirits. There is nothing like greed to turn a man's heart." Alvarez frowned back, plainly perplexed. "In this palace there is gold, all kinds of gold—solid bars, pure gold coins, heavy bracelets and necklaces and precious jewels of every kind."

"Yes, inside Montezuma's throne room," Alvarez agreed.

"Let our soldiers take all of it divide it up among themselves, as much as each man can carry on himself and in his saddlebags. They leave here alive and they will be rich men. That will make them fight their way out of here as they have never fought before," Cortes said as his eyes peered out beyond the square, seeing the Indians move back toward the buildings. The last of the day was fading away, he noted. "We may not have to fight at all," Cortes said. "It will be night soon. The Aztecs must sleep. They are human. They must be exhausted. But we will leave while they sleep, move out of this cursed place in the dead of night." He pointed through the gathering dusk to the vast lake that surrounded the city. "We will use the Tacuba Causeway," Cortes said.

"It is over a mile long," Alvarez reminded him.

"Yes, but still the shortest of them all," Cortes said, then strode away to where his soldiers had dismounted and rested. He quickly told his men they were free to pillage the palace, and he smiled as he watched them rush into the throne room. Alvarez's voice broke into his thoughts and he returned to the general, who pointed into the distance. Cortes immediately saw the Aztecs in canoes alongside the causeway.

"They are removing the bridge across the largest gap in the causeway," Alvarez said. "That ends your plan to escape."

"Not at all," Cortes answered. "It will present one more problem, but one we can solve. We have enough wood. We'll lay our own bridge across the gap. In one way, it is a good sign."

"How?" Alvarez asked.

"They'll be certain now that they have us trapped here. They'll really sleep and tonight, when the night is deep, they'll pay the price for their overconfidence. When they wake come morning, we will be gone," Cortes said. "Have the Tlaxcalans start bringing flat wood pieces for our bridge. Our broadswords can cut the pegs to keep the pieces together."

Alvarez hurried away and Cortes let a feeling of confidence take hold of him. No horde of inferior people were going to defeat the conquistadores, no matter how many of them there were, Cortes told himself. It never occurred to him that he, too, might pay the price for overconfidence. He smiled as he watched his soldiers return from the inner palace laden down with gold bars, chains, necklaces, and bejeweled objects, some carrying so much they could barely walk. He sat down against a wall and allowed himself to indulge in a few hours' sleep.

When he awoke, the slabs of wood had been brought, and Cortes supervised the cutting of the pegs to form a wide-enough single piece to bridge the causeway gap. The night had grown deeper. Outside there was a blanket of silence that had wrapped itself around the land. Cortes listened and heard not a voice, not a sound of any kind. The living slept as silently as the mounds of the dead. He began to prepare his men to steal out of Tenochtitlan. He had them remove all their leg and lower body armor that rubbed and clanked, letting them wear only their one-piece breastplates. Next, every horse's hooves were carefully wrapped in cloth so they'd make no sound as they moved across the stone of the causeway. Lastly, rein chains were tightened and silenced, the wheels of the falconets also covered with cloth.

With Cortes at the head of the column, the besieged Spaniards left the heart of the Aztec capital and began their silent march across the Tacuba Causeway. They moved slowly, every man aware of the need for silence. They also moved slowly, weighted down with the plunder they carried. The barefoot mercenaries moved silently in fear, aware of how few of their number were still alive. Cortes carefully led the way across the causeway, grateful for the wispy trails of fog that afforded a fitful cloak. But as he neared the gap in the causeway, the fog shredded in a freshening lake wind. Cortes ordered a halt and had his Indians slide the portable bridge into place, some lowering themselves into the water to do so. They had just positioned the makeshift bridge into place when all their best-laid plans shattered.

Some said it was a child lying awake, unable to sleep, who saw them. Some said it was a woman using the darkness to wash herself in the lake. Others said it was a figure that rose from the mountains of dead bodies, a kind of macabre miracle made to happen by divine forces. Whoever or whatever it was, someone saw the stealthy procession and cried out in the silent night. In seconds, from all over, the deep sound of conch shells being blown raised the alarm. In seconds more, the night exploded with the swarm of Aztecs that attacked from every part of the city. They attacked, some swimming across the water, some in canoes, and still more streaming onto the causeway from behind the Spaniards and from in front of them.

They came from every direction, filling the night with their wild shouts of rage. In hundreds of canoes, they attacked the portable bridge, ignoring long gun and cannon fire, two carrying on for every one that fell to the Spaniards' fire. Cortes saw his makeshift bridge being pulled down and sent his black stallion racing forward. He managed to cross over the bridge onto the other side. Not more than a dozen of his men were able to follow him over before the bridge was pulled into the water by the attackers. He saw the main part of his force beset upon from every direction by the Aztecs, many bare-handed but most using their wooden axes, knives, clubs, and long wooden spears. Many of the soldiers leaped into the water to swim the gap to the other end of the causeway only to find they were so weighed down by the gold and jewels they carried, that they drowned or were easily caught by their attackers.

Trapped on the short part of the causeway, the majority of Cortes's army was wiped out. In their frenzy of fury and victory, and in keeping with their ancient practice of human sacrifice, many cut the hearts out of the fallen Spaniards while tossing the others into the lake. Cortes sent his stallion into a full gallop along the causeway, followed by the few who had managed to get across with him. With his own fury and superior weapons, he fought his way through every knot of attackers until he reached the land at the end of the causeway. He saw he had but six men still with him, and he kept his horse running until it refused to run any longer.

The Aztecs, all on foot, stopped trying to pursue, content with finishing off any of the invaders still left alive. Cortes and his pitifully few men pressed their horses on, only halting when the dawn came. The *Noche Triste* was over. The Sad Night had come to an end. The conquistadores had been conquered. They were no longer messengers from the great God Quetzalcoatl. They no longer wore the mantle of divinity.

The Aztecs had shown for all other Indian peoples of the Mexican peninsula to see, that the Spanish were human and nothing more, their only power that of their weapons. And they had shown that the conquistadores could be vanquished. They were not invincible. No longer would Indian rulers bow to these plumed and armored invaders. No longer would they offer obeisance or gifts of gold and women. That night had changed the future. From then on, the Spanish would be offered only hostility and death, except for what corruption could buy them. That sad night was the beginning of many sad nights for the conquistadores. It was a turning point in history.

But it was not an end.

The Spanish had a foothold in this new land. They were not about to relinquish it. They replaced the disgraced Cortes with one Francisco Vasquez de Coronado. His mission was not only to conquer and gather riches, but to restore and repair the name, authority, and reputation of the conquistadores.

But the Aztecs were making their own plans for survival. To insure this, they called on the powers of the Golden One. Over three hundred years later, those powers found a new echo.

2

The big man astride the magnificent Ovaro shook the rain from the brim of his hat, his handsome, chiseled features drawn tight. "Don't like this," he muttered aloud. For two days he had been riding in grayness and rain, the sky a ceiling of slate, the ground turned muddy, the trees that covered the hills dulled of their vibrant verdant hue. But it wasn't just a gray day. It was that particular ominous gray that warned of a terrible promise. The rain was steady and growing heavier. But the jet black fore- and hindquarters and the pure white midsection of the Ovaro refused to bow to the grayness, the horse's muscles glistening in the rain.

Skye Fargo glanced down at the rivulets of water that coursed alongside the Ovaro's hoofs. They continued to grow deeper and wider. Fargo swore silently as he felt the apprehension stab at him. The land dipped down into a low, wide, valleylike stretch between the Cane River on one distant flank, and Six-gun Peak on the other. He'd ridden land such as this often enough, land made for trouble in sustained heavy rains. Halting, he swung from the saddle and knelt down, pressing his fingers into the ground. He allowed a grunt of satisfaction. Only the topsoil moved at his touch, the bottom soil still absorbing the rain. He gave thanks for good, healthy soil, with strong grass roots and plenty of nutrients holding it in place.

But that wouldn't last forever, he knew. Torrential rain would decimate even the best soil, overwhelming its ability to absorb any more water. Rainwater would become floodwater—the recipe for disaster. Returning to the saddle, Fargo rode on, hoping against hope that the gray sky would part. He moved past rows of cottonwoods filled with redwings, horned larks, and Bullock's orioles crowded into the shelter of the wide, triangular leaves. Following the instructions Julie had sent him long ago, he found the two intertwined bluejack oaks, their branches knotted together, then he turned north and rode into increasing rain and wind as he let his thoughts settle on his destination, a very special old friend called Julie Neemeyer. Julie had come to the lower Colorado country with her father, who had spent a lifetime raising sheep. When her pa was killed in an accident, Julie stayed, taking the sheep-raising business on for herself. According to her letters, she'd been able to make at least a modest living for herself.

That much didn't surprise him. Julie always had a core of quiet determination inside her. His visit to her was long, long overdue, Fargo grunted with regret this time. Julie had always known how to be a friend as well as a lover, a feat many women never managed to accomplish. Something inside Julie made you feel passion and protectiveness, lust and loyalty. Perhaps because she offered those qualities herself. They had been good lovers and good friends and Fargo remembered every day with Julie as a good day, whatever it happened to be. Fargo turned from his thoughts and eyed the sky again. The grayness allowed no lengthening afternoon shadows with which to measure the day, but he knew the afternoon had to be nearing an end. He went on another half mile, peering ahead against the curtain of rain, when he suddenly made out gray-white forms spread out in front of him.

He slowed, and the forms became sheep as he drew closer, one large flock staying together as sheep tend to do. He saw a second flock off to one side, also clustered together, then a third group to the left. Passing close to the first flock, he saw they were thoroughly wet but it was also plain that the rain hadn't penetrated their thick, tight, dense coats. He saw a small flock with sense enough to gather under a series of wide-roofed, open-sided shelters. A house appeared just beyond the shelters, low and sturdy with a good slate roof and solid side beams. A large barn alongside it held two cows—Holsteins, Fargo saw—a sow and a half-dozen piglets and scattered chickens.

He drew up to the house and the door opened as he swung from the horse. He saw her eyes go to the Ovaro at once, staring at it for a long moment. "By God, I don't believe it," she breathed. "By God, tell me I'm not dreaming."

"You're not," Fargo said as he pulled off his rain slicker. Julie was against him in seconds, her arms wrapped around him.

"You're here. You're really here," she breathed, holding tightly on to him.

"We're getting wet," he said and she pulled him into a modest living room with a fireplace, quilted rugs, a worn sofa, two easy chairs, and a puncheon table against one wall. He brought his eyes to Julie as she stood before him. She hadn't changed much. The years had been good to her, her rosy-cheeked face still holding its youthfulness, her brown eyes clear and her thick hair pulled back. He'd always called Julie a semiblonde. When she spent a lot of time in the sun, her hair turned a dark yellow that reverted to its usual light brown shade in the fall. Her figure seemed much the same as he remembered it; ample hips, her waist a little thicker, her breasts always pillowy without a great deal of shape, still filling her shirt with their fullness. Julie had always been more pleasant-faced than pretty, her features even, her mouth wide, an open sweetness that hadn't changed.

The lips that came to his also held the soft, warm sensualness he remembered. "You wrote you'd be coming but I didn't dare believe it," Julie said.

"Sorry it took me so long, Julie," he told her.

"You picked terrible weather," she said. "How long have you been riding in it?"

"Two days," he said as she took his arm, holding it tight.

"Got some good venison stew in the kettle. A bottle

of bourbon, too. This is going to be a celebration," Julie said.

"Anything I can help you with? The sheep need tending?" Fargo asked.

"They'll fend for themselves. Eventually, they all find their way under the overhangs," Julie said.

"I couldn't get much of a look at them in this downpour," Fargo said. "What have you got?"

"Mostly Devon and Lincoln, for now. I've plans on hold at the moment. But there's plenty of time to talk sheep. I want to talk about you and me and old times, and then not talk at all," Julie said, a sly little smile edging her lips. "Stable your Ovaro in the barn and bring your gear back here," she said and walked to the door with him. "I was getting so tired of this rain. Now I'll be remembering it for always," she said as he hurried outside and led the horse into the barn, hoping Julie's words weren't going to be prophetic in the wrong way.

Darkness slid over the land as he finished stabling the horse, and he returned to the horse through rain that continued to pour down heavily. Julie had brushed her hair and donned a pink shirt that clung tightly to her round breasts. "I've an extra room you can bed down in," she said. "And I'll be shooting you if you do," she added.

"Wouldn't want that." He laughed as they sat down to eat. The stew was delicious, the bourbon perfect, and when the meal was over and the rain still pounded hard against the windows, Julie led him to her bed. She flung off her shirt and skirt, then her slip.

"Am I being shameless?" she questioned.

"If so, I like it," he said and she waited, letting him take her in, plainly pleased with herself. She had a right to be, Fargo decided. The years had been good to her. She'd put on a little weight, her waist a little thicker, thighs a little heavier, breasts a little deeper, but their very red, large nipples and small areolas were still as enticing. The extra weight was distributed evenly, her skin still soft and smooth, clear of wrinkles. He shed his own clothes as she pulled him onto the wide bed with her.

"I've thought about this moment for so long. Never gave up hoping it'd come about and now it has," Julie said.

"Then stop talking." Fargo smiled, leaning down and bringing his mouth to her soft, warm lips. Julie's lips had a way of kissing and sucking at the same time, a totally seductive sensation. His hand moved over one round, pliant breast and she gasped. The gasp became a drawn-out cry as his mouth slid down to caress one deep red nipple.

"Oh, oh, ah . . ." Julie cried out, and he felt her hips twist one way then the other, wanton desire spreading through her. Little breathless explosions of pleasure rose from her as his lips explored her soft, luscious mounds, his tongue caressing her high-standing nipples and the sweet softness of her skin. His hand slowly slid downward, and Julie trembled as he touched the fleshy curve of her belly, moving down further to the little fold of skin just beneath it. Her hips twisted again as he reached the shaggy black

23

triangle of hair below, pressing through the unruly tuft that covered her Venus mound. The sensation stirred him; flocculent, soft yet wiry. "Oh, God, yes, yes, yes . . . oh, yes," Julie gasped, swinging her body around to lay atop him.

The warmth of her mound pressed down hard against his pulsating maleness. The clock turned back again as Fargo remembered how Julie had a way of enveloping him. Her full-fleshed thighs moved upward to press tightly around his hips and her torso seemed to cover him like a vibrant, sensual blanket. She moved against him, rubbing her downy triangle over his groin, and he felt her warm moisture against his pole. He lifted her up over his eager member and he felt her torrid wetness flow over him as he filled her eager, throbbing portal. Julie's head flew backward, her neck arched, and Fargo felt her sweet contractions against his rock-hard erectness. Her scream filled the room as she rode atop him, thrusting down and up and down again, her body twisting as she strove to absorb every moment of pleasure.

He stayed with her, lifted upward to match her shuddering thrusts as she tried to extract more than flesh and pleasure could give. She leaned the upper part of her body forward, rubbing her pendulous breasts into his face as her screams continued to fill the night. Suddenly, he felt her freeze as if she were seized, and she seemed to stop breathing. The warm flesh of her belly drew away from him sharply as her entire body grew taut. It was but a split second, yet she seemed suspended in space, and then her scream rose to new heights, curling through the room, an un-abandoned cry made of pure ecstasy. She exploded into frenzied life again, her body thrashing against him, pounding into him as she quivered and strained, twisted and turned, trying to make her body one with his, flesh unto flesh, pleasure unto pleasure. He exploded with her until finally, the moment that was beyond holding spiraled away.

But Julie fought to hold it, half screaming, half crying, her entire body trembling, pressed against him until finally, with a wrenching sob, she lay still atop him. Only an occasional twitch of her body gave proof that she hadn't fainted. He gently rolled her onto her back as he stayed inside her, and she gave a grateful whimper. Her eyes stayed closed a long time and when she finally opened them, she stared right up at him. "That's what happens when you stay away so long." She pouted and then let a little smile come to her lips. "It was everything I've waited for," she said, wriggling to make a little place for herself against his arm and broad chest. "I'm going to sleep now," Julie murmured.

He smiled and remembered how that had always been a part of their lovemaking. He watched her close her eyes, her face wreathed in contentment, and in moments she was fast asleep. As always in the past, she drew one leg over his groin, her body asserting its own possessiveness. Fargo lay awake, listening to the pounding of the rain on the roof until he, too, closed his eyes and slept. When morning came, he woke to the soft rustle of sheets and a glimpse of Julie's attractively plump rear disappearing into the other room. He rose, found a large basin of water and a washcloth, and when he was dressed, he followed the smell of biscuits into the small kitchen. Julie turned, coffeepot in hand. The way her breasts swayed under a loose, one-piece dress told him she had nothing on beneath it. Her body pressed sensuously against his as she kissed him good morning confirmed his suspicion.

"Sit down, coffee's ready," she said. He paused to peer out the window and felt his jaw tighten.

"No sign of it letting up," he said.

"We often get heavy rains here. Keeps my grass tall and fresh for the sheep," Julie said.

"Heavy as this?" he asked.

She let a moment of concern touch her face. "No, this is more than I've ever seen," she conceded as he drew a sip of the bracing, fresh brew. She held on to her confidence, he saw. Perhaps because she knew there was nothing else to hold on to. He'd not take that from her, he told himself, but he'd not let her pay the ultimate price for it.

"Can I help with anything this morning? Feeding sheep?" he asked.

"They won't be fed till this afternoon," she said. "I've some wool to put into bundles, but you can't help me with that. I need to sort out the best from the next best and so on."

"You're right there. I wouldn't know one strand from another," Fargo said.

"Soon as the storm stops, I'll be getting visits from my regular customers," Julie said.

"Sounds as though you're making out, then," Fargo remarked.

"So far. Got some good customers who come all the way from Cañon City and Colorado Springs," Julie said with pride. "They like my wool."

"You handle all this by yourself?" Fargo questioned.

"No. I've three shearers who come once a month, and two general hands come by once a week," Julie said. "And I'm making plans. If it's a good year, I'll have enough money to expand my flocks."

"Expand?"

"Add some Cotswold and Cheviot, and maybe a small herd of Jacob. They'll give me wool no one in a dozen states around here has. Of course, that'll take a sizeable investment," Julie said as she sat on his lap.

"I'm glad for you, Julie. Kind of proud, too," Fargo said.

"And now you've come visiting. That makes everything perfect," she said.

He squeezed her and stood up. "Do your bundles. I'll be back in time to help you feed," he said.

She frowned at him. "Why are you going out in this weather?" she questioned.

"Just to look around some. I get nervous in this kind of downpour," he said.

"Skye Fargo, you don't know the meaning of the word nervous," Julie tossed back. "Now, if you don't want to tell me what takes you out in this terrible

27

weather, that's your right. But you better make up a better story than being nervous."

"Got to go visit another gal I promised to make happy," he said evenly.

"Now that I can believe," she said. "Just get back by afternoon."

"Promise," he said and she clung to him, her lips meeting his. He then donned his rain gear and went to the stable. Julie knew he'd explain his actions when he was ready. Trust and understanding had always been a part of their relationship. He rode from the barn, seeing that most of the sheep had finally gathered under the open-sided roofed shelter. As he rode, he swore silently as he felt the Ovaro's hooves sink deeper into the ground. The undersoil was saturated and the rainwater now lay six inches deep on the ground. As he rode, he studied the water and saw that it moved ever so slowly, pushing in from the north.

That meant only one thing: There was a runoff from higher land. Not from Six-gun Peak, though. Not yet. When the water came down from the peak it would be a racing torrent. Following the movement of the groundwater, wiping the rain from his eyes every few moments, Fargo finally discerned the dark gray outline of a ridgeline, and sent the Ovaro toward it. He came to a ridge of rock running in long, horizontal steps. Following a narrow passageway, he steered the Ovaro through water that rushed almost knee-high around the horse's legs. The passage opened up onto another horizontal ridge and exploring further, Fargo found a third level of granite ridges. Woolly lipferns clung to the underside of rocky ledges, surviving where no other plant could. A last and fourth ridge looked down over the land below from some forty feet up, he guessed, more than high enough to afford a life-saving perch.

Exploring even further, he found a long rock overhang, large enough to be dry in the furthermost part. Fargo turned the Ovaro and began to make his way down the water-filled passages. It was near the morning's end when he rode back over the low land and saw that the water level had risen since he'd crossed this way. Though it was too far away to see, even without the deluge, he knew the Cane River had to be approaching its flood stage. It wasn't wide or deep enough to absorb much more of this kind of unceasing rain. A glance at the sky showed unending rainclouds. When he reached Julie's place, he stabled the Ovaro, pausing to glance at a roan mare she had in the barn, seeing it was a sturdy animal.

Julie looked up as he entered. "She wasn't home," he said blandly and ducked a cushion that flew at him.

"Don't take off your rain gear. It's time to feed," she said and slipped on a long slicker that covered her from head to toe. Julie had Fargo help her carry sacks of grain and some half bales of hay, which they distributed among the flocks. They put the grain into low, shallow troughs. "In good weather I'd pour it on the ground and let them forage for it but it'd be all washed away in this weather," Julie said. Next she had him help her herd the sheep on the outer edges of the flocks into the center so they could get some of the feed. The sheep were very wet, Fargo noted as he ran his hands over them, but only on the surface of their coats. Their dense, thick fleece absorbed and shed the rain with astonishing efficiency.

"What do you do about wolves?" Fargo asked Julie as he hoisted another half bale of hay and began to spread it out.

"I've been lucky. Wolves have been scarce, but lately I've seen more of them coming closer. I'm going to get me some big guard dogs—Great Pyrenees. They're bred for guarding sheep," she said as they finished spreading the feed. It had been time-consuming and the afternoon was drawing to a close as they finished and returned to the house. Before he went inside, Fargo glanced back, his eyes measuring the water depth as it lay atop the ground. Inside, he fought down the urge to share his alarm with Julie. She was all happiness and stubborn optimism. Perhaps that was enough to work miracles. He'd not destroy that possibility, so he stayed silent.

Dinner was a necessary delay on the way to her bed, and after eating, Julie brought all her full-fleshed softness to him once again. She rubbed her wide, supple breasts across his body, from his thighs up across his groin. Lingering there, she moaned with the excruciating pleasure of sensation. Finally, she slid herself further upward until her erect red tips found his mouth. She pressed deep and moaned at the beauty that was taste and touch. His hands explored downward, and found her waiting, wanton wetness. Julie twisted as she screamed out, her every cry growing louder with every new exercise in ecstasy. Her passion soared higher than the night before and the room echoed with scream after scream as she twisted and turned, rose and fell back, surged and drew away only to surge again. In the dim glow of the lone candle, Fargo felt his own desires explode at the beauty of her wild wanting, immersing himself in her body, the touch of her unruly triangle, her fleshy thighs, her sweet tunnel of ecstasy.

But finally, her every sense exhausted, she slept against him with that complete contentment that came with satisfying lovemaking. The night had grown deep and he slept with her softness enveloping around him, until his wilderness-honed, innate hearing yanked him into wakefulness. Lying still, he listened, letting the sound sort itself out in his mind. It came from outside the window—the sound of rain still hammered on, but there was a subtle change to it. Sliding away from Julie without waking her, Fargo went to the window and peered out, but the moonless night let him see only blackness. He took the candle and held it up to the window and the oath fell from his lips. Setting the candle down, he woke Julie.

She took a moment to awake, staring up at him. "Get dressed, put on your boots and all your rain gear," he said. She swung from the bed as he helped pull her up, and began to dress with alarm in her round-cheeked face. Fargo threw on clothes and was dressed before she finished. "What is it?" Julie asked.

"We're getting out of here. The barn and the horses, first," Fargo said.

"Why?" she asked as he pulled her along with him, moving to open the front door. Julie gave a half cry as the water rushed in with a bubbling fury, reaching their knees in seconds. It settled some as it swept into the house and Fargo led Julie outside, pushing his way to the barn. While he saddled the Ovaro, Julie threw her gear onto the roan. He opened the stalls for the cows as she finished.

"They'll have to fend for themselves," he muttered, and pulled himself onto the Ovaro and rode from the barn. Julie rode beside him, seeing that the rising water had already reached the horses' hocks. The Cane had flooded, spilling over its banks and across the low land. But the way the water swirled told him that Six-gun Peak was pouring water down in a torrent, as well. He spurred the Ovaro, pushing forward through the eddying water and saw the pain on Julie's face as she threw a glance at the sheep. Most were still standing huddled together. Sheep were not known as good swimmers, certainly not in raging floodwaters. Fargo reached out, grabbed hold of the roan's cheekstrap, and pulled her along with him. Saving Julie was his only goal, the only one possible. The water was rising too fast. The horses would be swimming soon, he saw, but he kept the Ovaro driving forward, trying to gain another few dozen yards in distance and a few precious seconds of time.

When he felt the horse begin to swim, Fargo slid from the saddle and, holding on to the saddle horn, swam alongside his mount. Julie followed and clung to the side of the roan, but her eyes cut to Fargo, despair and the realization of disaster stark in her face. "It's no use," she said. "It's rising too fast. The current's too strong."

"Keep going!" he shouted back. "There's a place we'll be safe. We just have to reach it." He had drawn a bead on the ridge in his mind when they rode from the barn, and now he guided the Ovaro to the right, adjusting their course and cursing as he felt the floodwater's current pulling at him. He also felt the Ovaro tiring, and his own legs began to turn to lead when he managed to discern the darker shape directly ahead of him. The land rose as he neared the rock ridgeline, and finally he saw the horse touch ground and begin to step forward instead of swim. He swung onto the saddle and motioned to Julie. "Mount up," he said and she pulled herself onto the roan.

The rising waters continued to press at them but the horses stepped quickly on land as it sloped upward. The horizontal ridges were now distinct. The bottom step already lay underwater, but Fargo found the passageway that led upward, helping guide the Ovaro onto the next ridge and halting to wait for Julie. The floodwaters were already lapping at the second ridge and Fargo guessed it, too, would be underwater in less than fifteen minutes. He probed his way until he found the next narrow crevice that snaked its way upward to the third ridge. When he found it, he moved along the ridge line until he came to the deep overhang. Julie rode to the rear behind him. He dismounted and helped her from the roan as the soft, lapping sounds of the rising floodwaters drifted up to where they were.

"So *this* is what you were doing riding out in the rain," Julie said.

"Figured we'd need a place. I hope I guessed right about the water not rising this high," he said.

"If you didn't?" she asked.

"We're in a lot of trouble," Fargo said. "If it keeps rising, it'll sweep us right off of here." He didn't need to finish. Julie's grave face told him she understood.

"How long before we know?" she asked.

"Not long," he said, listening to the sound of the water against the rocks just below them. They sat side by side at the back of the overhang where it was still dry, until Fargo rose and walked to the front of the ridge. His lips pulled back in a grimace as he saw how close the floodwaters had come to the top of the ledge. Just as a bird is transfixed by the eyes of the snake before it, he stood staring at the water as it continued to rise. In hardly minutes, it swirled to less than two inches from the lip of the ledge, still rising. Once it overflowed the ledge, it would rush back to the rear of the overhang and sweep them out into the flood.

They could take to the horses, but he knew that neither horses nor humans would last long in the torrential swirl of the floodwaters. Suddenly he felt Julie beside him, her fingers twining into his.

He held her but his eyes stayed on the water, watching it climb closer—less than an inch from the top now,

34

he saw with his own rising tide of bitterness. He had hoped the high ridge would keep them safe, but he had been wrong. The floodwaters were about to make him pay for that error as they refused to be cheated. But it had been the only place to offer them any chance of survival in the low land. He threw a last angry glance at the water that crept ever closer to the top of the ledge, and started to turn to get back on the horses. If he were going to drown, he'd do so in the saddle along with his friend and companion for so many years. Turning, he halted, his ears catching the almost susurrant sound.

He looked back at the floodwaters, so close to the edge of the ridge, now. But they weren't rising. Fargo frowned down at the dark, swirling spectre of death. The floodwaters stayed in place, rushing past just underneath the top of the ledge. Fargo was almost afraid to believe his eyes. He stared as the waters stayed in place. "It's stopped," he breathed in awe and grateful relief. "It's stopped. We made it." He drew his arm around Julie as she trembled against him.

"You sure?" she asked.

"Yes." He nodded. "When it stops rising that means it's topped out."

"Good God, oh, good God," Julie murmured, her voice breaking. She stared down at the floodwaters as she clung to him, finally found her voice again. "How long will it take to go down?" she asked.

"That depends on a lot of things. How much runoff space is available. How much sun we get. The condition of the land. Different soils absorb water at different rates. But it won't be overnight," he told her, and led her back to the dry section of the overhang. He took a large blanket from his saddlebag and started to undress. "Get your clothes off," he said and she hurried to shed her wet garments. When she was naked with him, their clothes spread out on the dry stone of the ledge, he wrapped the blanket around them both and lay down with her.

Julie held her body tight against him with a new fervency. "Make me forget what's happened, Fargo, if only for a little while. Make me forget," she murmured.

He obeyed and the rocky overhang echoed her screams of passion that were filled not only with pleasure, but an attempt to erase the watery world around them. They reverberated from the silent rocks until finally she grew still and he felt her sleeping against him. The worst of the swirling flood was over, but not the worst of what it would leave behind, Fargo knew, as he closed his eyes and slept, entwined inside the blanket with Julie. They were alive, and he wondered if that was the only thing Julie would have to hold on to when the floodwaters receded.

Fargo was certain of only one thing: Her tomorrows would carry pain and despair. But he had no way of knowing that another time, over three hundred years earlier, would echo all the way to those very tomorrows.

3

Francisco Vasquez de Coronado surveyed the expeditionary force he had assembled and allowed himself a smile of satisfaction. A tall, slender man with a goatee that never grew beyond wispiness, Coronado carried even more arrogance than his fellow conquistadores. After all, it was he who had been chosen after the Aztec defeat of Cortes, to restore the power and the prestige of Spain in the new lands. But he knew that was not an easy assignment. No longer could the conquistadores strike fear by their very presence. Now they were seen simply as invaders. The Aztecs had done that. The Aztecs had shown that the Spanish were only human and vulnerable. And so, the message had come all the way from distant Spain: Punish the Aztecs and pillage the land.

This was Coronado's twin goal, destroy the Aztecs and loot everything from everyone else. As he exhorted his officers and troops, he spoke of the information the Spanish had wrought with torture and gold. "Their most powerful rulers prepare to run," Coronado said. "But they will not run. We will follow wherever they go, track them down until we kill every last one of them. We will make an example of them for all others to see." A swelling chorus of cheers interrupted him. "And along the way we will send more gold and riches back than the mother country has ever seen," Coronado went on. "Even now, the Seven Cities of Cibola wait for us like plums to be plucked from a tree. It is said that their very houses are made of gold and shine in the sun. The good Friar Marcos has seen this with his very eyes. At the end of our mission, each of you will be rich."

Longer and louder cheers rose from his listeners as Francisco Vasquez de Coronado raised one arm and sent his army forward. He watched, entirely pleased with herself. He commanded a force of over three hundred twenty-five armored horsemen, five hundred Indian mercenaries, six hundred extra horses, and five hundred hogs and goats for food along the march. He had further arranged for squads of mercenaries, commanded by units of his armored knights, to carry the gold and other precious items they would seize back to command quarters while he continued to pursue the Aztecs. Completely confident, he swung his horse up to the head of the long column and proceeded north.

But word of Coronado's plans was carried to the Aztecs before the general had even begun his march. They began to lay their own plans, not so much for battle as for survival. They knew all too well how many thousands and thousands of their people they had lost, and they knew the invaders would come with even more men, and even more weapons. They knew there was a time to stand and a time to flee, a time to offer sacrifice and a time to plan survival. A new king had replaced the disgraced and fallen Montezuma, and his name was Cuauhtemoc. On a dark night, Cuauhtemoc called together his advisors and high priests and a special group of specially chosen warriors. Only a half circle of light shone from the fires lit behind the great carved stone monoliths that rose upward in the night.

Seated in front of the stone carvings, rows of nearly naked young men sat cross-legged. They were the cream of the Aztec people: the bravest, the strongest, the smartest—the best of the best.

"It will be different, this time," the new ruler warned. "They will not make the mistakes the one called Cortes made. They will not let themselves be trapped. They will stay in the open where they can charge with their horses and their mighty weapons. This new invader they call Coronado wants to destroy the Aztec people, to turn all of our sacred objects into dust. You have been chosen to make sure this does not happen. You have been chosen not only to survive, but to keep safe all of our sacred objects of wisdom and worship. If our sacred objects fall into the hands of the invaders, it will mean the end of our people."

One of the high priests rose and spoke to the young men. "Fight only when you must. There are others who will attack the invaders. Your mission is to flee, to keep our sacred objects from falling into the enemy's hands. Let them follow you to the end of the

Land of the Feathered Serpent, but never let them touch our sacred objects. In your hands will be everything on which are inscribed all the secrets of our wisdom—our writing, our medicine, our calendar. These are the very heart of our people, our being. These are the sacred icons entrusted to us by the great God Quetzalcoatl, from the smallest amulet to the great stone scrolls, from the chalices to the tablets. You have been given sacks, pouches, and slings to carry everything to safety."

Cuauhtemoc rose again and held up the first of the sacred objects, depositing it at the foot of the first row of young men. "I give you the very life of Aztec spirit. Take them all. Never let them fall into the hands of the invaders," he said. "And now, the dance of the golden one. By this dance, she will bestow upon you the special powers of protection the great god Quetzalcoatl had given her to give to others, and to you."

More wood was added to the fires and, moments later, a figure stepped from behind the great stone monoliths; a young woman clothed only in a green, silk garment. Long, jet black hair hung almost to her waist, framing a face of almost ethereal beauty, a face both proudly regal and boldly sensual. Her eyebrows arched high over steady, black eyes, and her high cheekbones were surprisingly wide in such a narrow face. With a slow, graceful motion, she pulled off the wispy garment and stood beautifully naked before them. The firelight danced across a body of perfect proportions, slender with narrow hips and long, gorgeous legs, breasts that fitted her body with magnificent curves that seemed to flow gently like a satin tide.

But it was her skin that echoed the name Cuauhtemoc had used . . . the Golden One.

In the firelight, her skin seemed flecked with gold so that she virtually glowed. Even standing still, she seemed surrounded by a golden aura. The sound of wooden flutes rose from the night, accompanied by conch shells in a variety of pitches and tones. Suddenly, the flutes and conch shells were accompanied by the surging beat and rhythm of goatskin drums. To the undulating music, she began to dance, and it was as though a figure of gold had come to life. Gleaming and glistening in the firelight, the young woman moved with sensuous beauty, swinging and swaying to the music. Her long, beautifully slender legs arched and turned, and her perfectly balanced breasts swayed in rhythm. Her jet black hair swirled around her as she danced, hiding and revealing her magnificent nakedness with tantalizing wildness. The music grew stronger, quicker, and the young woman began to whirl in a series of turns and dips until suddenly she was spinning so hard, it seemed her breasts were standing straight out from her body.

She spun harder and faster, harder and faster, until with an almost shocking abruptness, the music stopped and she collapsed onto the ground, her legs crossed, her head thrown back, a creature of golden magnificence. The high priest let her recapture her breath before he went to her, helping her to her feet as she glowed, even as the firelight began to fade. "The

Golden One has danced for you. In her dance she has given you all that the great god Quetzalcoatl has bestowed upon her. Her spirit is the spirit that has been handed down through the ages. Now she will pass on that spirit, and those powers, in one more way that is part of her heritage." Turning to the young woman, he gestured to the rows of chosen warriors at her feet. "Select the one you wish and finish the sacred dance."

The young woman moved down the rows of the waiting warriors, walking slowly in all her naked beauty, and finally chose one. She disappeared into the darkness beyond the firelight with him and the night grew silent. But finally, a long, shuddered cry of fulfillment rose to spiral through the darkness. The high priest stepped forward once again. "It is finished," he intoned. "The gift of the Golden One has been given and will live on as it is written in the prophecies."

Cuauhtemoc motioned for the young men to rise with him. "Day will come soon. You will begin your sacred mission with the first sun. The spirit and the heritage of the Aztec people go with you." With those last words, the ruler and his high priests majestically walked from the circle. Little more than an hour passed before the sun's first rays slanted across the land. The warriors began their flight north. But many of the things they carried were heavy, and they had no horses to bear the loads. It was a slow and hard trek, but they moved forward nonetheless, conserving their energy as much as they could for the arduous journey ahead.

Meanwhile, Coronado, moving with the information given him by spies and informants, had set a forced march through the night. He sent most of his horsemen on ahead and when dawn rose, they were not far behind the fleeing Aztecs.

4

Fargo woke to a full, hot sun and a bright, cloudless day in which Mother Nature blithely ignored the fury and devastation she had loosed. He dressed in clothes now dry and stood at the front of the ridge as Julie came to stand beside him. The floodwaters still covered the land, deep, still, and quietly dangerous, but they were receding with surprising speed. "Good runoff someplace," Fargo commented.

"How long before we can go back down?" Julie asked.

"Maybe by the end of the day," Fargo said, seeing the sober concern wreathing Julie's face. He returned to the rear of the ridge, unsaddled the Ovaro, and took out his grooming kit from his saddlebag. "Unsaddle the mare. She'll need cleaning, too," he told Julie. Using the dandy brush, the sweat scraper, and the stable rubber for the final polishing, he groomed the Ovaro while Julie worked on the roan alongside him. The horses needed the residue of the floodwaters cleaned from their coats and besides, Fargo knew it would occupy Julie's thoughts, if only for a while.

They worked leisurely, and the day was drawing toward an end when they finished. His guess had been a good one, he saw, as he surveyed the land again below the ridge. The waters had receded far enough for them to start the ride down and when Fargo squinted into the distance he saw why. At the far end of the lowland, a valley dipped even lower, providing a giant sluice that spilled out below the high land of Six-gun Peak. With Julie beside him, Fargo began to move down the ridge. The drenched land sucked at the horses' hooves and water still lay some three feet deep when they reached the lowland. Fargo kept his face impassive as pieces of furniture floated by, followed by the open shell of a trunk. A child's cradle followed, then scraps of assorted clothing and the bloated bodies of a half-dozen hogs. Julie's face drew tight, her lips pressed into a thin line.

"There were other houses down at the bottom of the valley," she said glumly. Her shoulders sagged further with every drowned, dead animal and water-logged object that floated past. Fargo wanted to help her, find words that would comfort her, but he knew there weren't any and he rode with a feeling of terrible helplessness. Only the soft, splashing sound of the horses' hooves broke the silence as they rode across the increasingly littered lowland. They were nearing her place when he spotted the white expanse, mound-like in shape, that they soon saw were sheep, still huddled together in death as they lay on their sides.

He saw one group, then another, and still another a dozen yards on. He threw a glance at Julie. She sat very straight in the saddle, her face impassive, but then he saw the two lines of tears running down her cheeks. The house came into sight next. It was still standing, water still pouring out of the open door. Julie pulled to a halt. Her voice would have been calm if it weren't for the quiver in it.

"Guess it'll take a few more days drying out before I can start to clean it up," she murmured. He moved the Ovaro against the roan, reached over, and pulled her from the horse, and held her in the saddle with him as her grief burst open, weeping openly into his chest. He held her as her sobs wracked her body until finally they subsided. "Finished . . . everything finished," she murmured.

"You'll have to start over, find higher ground this time," Fargo said.

"Start over?" Julie echoed. "With what? I've no sheep and I haven't the money to buy new flocks. The price of good stock has tripled."

"What about the bank?" Fargo tried.

"I still owe them from the last flock," Julie said. Fargo felt thoughts quietly forming inside him.

"You can't stay here. Got anywhere to go for a few days?" he asked.

"Agnes Covingham in Temple Rock will put me up," Julie said.

"If it's not underwater," Fargo said.

"Shouldn't be. Temple Rock's up on the high plateau," she said.

"Let's find out," Fargo said and helped swing her

back onto the roan. He started to turn the Ovaro around.

"No, not that way," Julie said at once. "I can't look at them again. We'll go around the other way to town." He nodded, following her as she made a wide circle through the water, reaching land that began to climb upward. They were out of the water before he saw the buildings of the town rise in front of him. The high plateau was just high enough to have been spared, but he saw the high watermark where the flood had reached. Nearing the town, he saw the crowds of other refugees making their way to Temple Rock, their wagons hauling in possessions that had survived the flood. His eyes glanced at the tall piece of sandstone that rose and arched at one side of the town and had obviously given the place its name. Julie led the way to the far end of town where a neat, white clapboard house faced the main street, a large store window taking up the right side of the building. Inside the window, wool jackets, coats, and scarves were on display. "From my wool," Julie said pridefully and he heard the sob catch in her throat.

Mrs. Covingham answered their knock. Fargo took in a large, white-haired woman with a ruddy, friendly face and long arms that pulled Julie into a warm embrace. "I was so worried about you, my child," the woman said. "But no one dared go down to the lowland while the flood was raging."

"I'm alive, thanks to my friend Fargo," Julie said and introduced him. He followed them into the house and into a comfortably furnished living room.

"You'll stay here, of course. For now, at least," Mrs. Covingham said to Julie. "You'll need time to get a handle on things."

"That'll mostly be burying carcasses," Julie said bitterly.

"Sit down while I get some coffee," the woman said and returned with cups and coffee in only a few minutes. "Just made it," she said. Fargo sat down, sipped his coffee, and let Julie and the woman talk while his thoughts began to crystallize further, each time he saw the pain in Julie's eyes. It wasn't until later, when Mrs. Covingham had gone to bed and he was alone with Julie, that he put thoughts into words.

"You'll have the money you need to buy new flocks and get a new place. I can get it for you," Fargo said.

"You can't do that." Julie frowned.

"I can and I will," Fargo replied.

"I can't let you," Julie said, and he put a finger on her lips.

"I want to," he said. "I'll be getting paid for it."

"I don't understand," Julie said.

"I had an offer just before coming to see you, a damn big offer. I didn't take it," Fargo said.

"Why not?"

"I was coming to see you. Didn't see any reason to change my plans," Fargo said. She leaned over and pressed her lips to his.

"Thank God," she murmured.

"You know me, Julie. I've always picked the jobs offered me, turning down as many as I've taken," Fargo said. "This was a strange offer. From a woman, and I don't really know what she wanted."

"Tell me about it, just as it happened," Julie said.

Fargo sat back, letting his thoughts return to that day in north Kansas.

"The job was over," he began. "A long, hard trail to break, all the way from Possum Kingdom in Texas to Big Smoky in Kansas for Ben Boardman's rotten, mean-tempered longhorns. Ben and I spent the weekend celebrating. I'd left a forwarding address. You know I often do that when I'm going to be on the trail a long time. I was in my hotel room, recovering from the celebration, when I had a visitor. I didn't want to see anyone. My head still pounded but I thought it might be Ben sending up another bottle of bourbon. I threw on some trousers and answered the door. The man standing there wasn't the hotel clerk and he wasn't holding a bottle of bourbon. He was fairly short, wearing an embroidered vest and wide, Mexican-style chaps, and he was carrying a six-shot, single-action French Navy Lefaucheux pistol. His black hair framed a broad, flat, olive-skinned face with dark, nervous eyes.

"Whoever you are, you've got the wrong room," I growled.

"The clerk told me I have the right room. You are Skye Fargo, the Trailsman," he said, a faint Mexican accent in his voice.

"Then you've the right room at the wrong time," I said but he kept his foot in the door. Drawing an envelope from inside his embroidered vest, he handed it to me.

"A message for you. I'll wait for you to read it," he said.

"I'll read it later," I said and he caught the change in my voice.

"I'll come back," he replied.

"Don't hurry," I said and he removed his foot from the door and hurried away.

I tossed the envelope on the bed and lay down beside it. I dozed for another few hours until the pounding in my head toned down to a dull throbbing. Finally, as night came, I lighted the lamp, washed, and pulled on clothes. The envelope refused to lose itself in the sheets and I sat down and opened it, seeing a brief note in a large, flowing script:

Mr. Skye Fargo,

I have a job for you that will pay you extremely well, too well to refuse. I am in Yucca Flats, Arizona territory, the only house on Cactus Lane. I shall expect you as soon as you receive this note.

Solita Chiltec

I put the note back into its envelope, aware that I'd already decided to turn it down. I didn't want to take on another job right away and I'd already decided to come see you. Besides, it had an air of command to it that was enough to turn me off. I was about to go to Ben's place when my visitor came back. I answered his knock and gave him back the envelope. "Tell the good lady she'll have to find someone else," I told him.

"She does not want someone else. She wants you," he said.

"She's not getting me. Good-bye," I said.

"Nobody turns down Solita Chiltec," he said.

"There's a first time for everything," I told him.

"This is a mistake on your part, a very big mistake," he said, his voice growing threatening.

"I've made them before. I'll make them again. Conversation over," I said and closed the door on him. His hard knock followed instantly. "I'm getting annoyed, sonny," I said.

"Solita Chiltec would want me to give you another chance," he said with a kind of menacing stiffness.

"That's nice. Don't come back," I said crossly and closed the door again. I heard him leave after a moment and I left the room soon after, went to the public stable, got my horse, and rode to Ben's place in plenty of time for dinner. Ben had a mixed-blood woman who cooked a fine meal and he produced a bottle of rare Pedro Ximenez Malaga. It became an evening of good food, good talk, and good liquor that lasted far too late into the night. When I finally rode back to the hotel I saw the one-horse spring wagon a few feet from the hotel entrance. I gave it a curious glance when a figure stepped out from behind it. I recognized the embroidered vest at once. As the man began to walk toward me I saw the pistol in his hand, raised and aimed at me. "What do you think you're doing?" I asked him.

"You wouldn't obey Solita Chiltec's letter so I am taking you back to her," he said. "I told you, no one refuses an order from Solita."

"Put that down before you get yourself seriously hurt, maybe killed," I told him with more impatience than anger.

"I know you are very fast with a gun. I know your reputation. But there are three men behind you. Their guns are aimed at you," he said. I half turned and the embroidered vest had been truthful abut that much. Two of the men held pistols, one a rifle. But I decided to make a bet on another kind of truth. I was betting my life on it, I realized. The three couldn't miss from that range. I turned back to the embroidered vest.

"Is that what the wagon's for, to take me back?" I asked.

"Yes. Carefully tied up, of course," he answered. "Now throw your gun down . . . very carefully."

It was time to make that bet, I told myself, not without a small qualm. Instead of throwing the Colt down, I took a step forward. "Stop . . . right there," the little man said, sudden alarm in his voice. I shifted my body sideways as I threw a looping left, just to be on the safe side. I was right. His gun went off as my blow landed and he went down. I felt the bullet whistle past me as I followed through, twisting the gun out of his hand and yanking him to his feet. I held him in front of me, the Colt pressed into his side and spun him around to face the other three.

"Drop the guns," I ordered. They took a moment but finally put their weapons down.

"You are a damned fool," the fancy vest said. "You take a very big chance. You were lucky."

"No chance. No luck," I said, stepping back and letting him turn around. He frowned back. "They didn't shoot because you told them not to," I said. The frown became a glare. "Your boss told you to bring me to her. I wouldn't do her any good dead," I said. His glare deepened as I laughed and my eyes flicked to the wagon and saw the coil of rope inside it. "Start tying one of them, hands and feet," I ordered. "Nice and tight." I watched as he began the task, making sure it was done properly. "Now the next one," I said and finally he finished tying the third man. I helped him lift the three men into the wagon when he finished and then I tied his hands and feet and tossed him into the wagon with the others.

The Ovaro followed along as I drove the wagon to Ben's place, where I borrowed two of his hands and had them drive the wagon and its cargo to Yucca Flats. I didn't send a note along, figured there was no need. The delivery would speak for itself. It was only two days later, when I was getting ready to come see you, that another note arrived, this one left with the hotel clerk. Curious, I read it at once:

Skye Fargo . . .
   My apologies for the behavior of those I sent to see you. Good intentions and poor judgment. My need for your services remains, my offer still a very lucrative one. I will wait for your visit.
                                        Solita Chiltec

The air of command had been softened, but it still lingered too much for me. I came to see you instead.

Fargo sat back, his story ended. "Lucky for me," Julie murmured.

"But things are different, now. I'll go see her and take her offer. You'll have the money you need," Fargo said.

"You'll get it back soon as my new flocks start producing wool," Julie said.

"Your way, your time," he told her.

A suddenly mischievous smile edged her lips. "For everything?" she murmured.

"For everything," he said.

Her lips found his and she made the night pass in her own way in her own time.

Proper goodbyes were said in the morning and Fargo rode south, then east in the bright, warm day. He set a steady pace and he didn't need a map, road signs, towns, or travelers to know when he'd left Colorado and entered the Arizona territory. The land spoke to him in its infinite ways, the dry feel of it under his horse's hooves, the gray-green expanse of distant brittlebrush, the soft yellow of a paloverde tree, a mourning dove nesting in a jumping cholla, a wolf spider burrow and the murkiness of shallow streams. But there was beauty marking the land, also; the sudden, deep red of a buckhorn cholla in bloom, the soft gold of a flowering barrel cactus.

Fargo swung the Ovaro to the east, riding with the distant high peaks of the Superstition Mountains to his right, keeping in a line of ironwood that afforded some shade from the hot sun. He was just climbing out of a dip in the land when he heard the voices, the sudden, sharp cry of a young woman's voice first, then the rough, angry voices of men. Fargo slowed, moving the horse through the trees and the figures soon came into sight. A girl and an older man stood near a buckboard, the girl in a green shirt and blue jeans, short-cut brown hair, and a square face with a stubborn line to it. The man near her had sparse hair and a considerable paunch. Five men surrounded them, two of them holding the older man. Fargo's eyes paused at the rope slung over a tree branch, a noose tied at the end of it. One of the men, heavy-set with a thick jaw, ordered, "Talk, girlie, or we'll hang him, sure as hell."

"Talk about what? We don't know anything. You've got the wrong people. You made a mistake, I keep telling you," the young woman said.

The men holding the older man dragged him to the lynching rope. "Enough talk. Let's get rid of them. That's all we're supposed to do, anyway," one of them said.

"Go ahead," the heavy-jawed one growled. "Then we'll enjoy her before we string her up." They started to put the rope around the older man's neck.

"No, wait!" the girl cried out.

"Don't bother, Clea," the older man said. "They're going to kill us both, whether you talk to them or not."

"Now, that's a terrible thing to say. We might let you go," the slack-jawed one said.

"Terrible and true, goddamn you," the older man said. Fargo nodded in silent agreement. These five were not the kind to show mercy. The two holding the older man moved quickly, slipping his head into the noose. "Last chance, girlie," the slack-jawed one said, and Fargo saw the girl's eyes lock on the older man, her face mirroring the anguish inside her.

"See you up with St. Peter, sweetie," the older man said. "It was almost a good ride."

Fargo swore silently. He had seen more than enough. But the two men were about to send the horse bolting out from underneath the doomed man in the saddle. There was time for only one shot, and it had to be on target. Fargo drew the Colt in one quick, smooth motion, aimed, and fired. The bullet hit the lynching rope as strands of hemp flew into the air. The rope parted just as the horse bolted forward. Fargo sent the Ovaro into the open as the five men turned in surprise. "Sorry to spoil your fun," Fargo said. "But then I never cared much for lynching parties."

"Son of a bitch," the slack-jawed one swore, then yanked his six-gun out to fire. The Colt barked again and he stiffened, staggered, and fell. His jaw fell open further as he twitched and lay still. The others stared at him for a moment, then yanked their own guns out. Fargo fired again and two more went down hard. The last two dived away, running and leaping onto their horses, staying flattened in their saddles as they raced away. Fargo didn't waste bullets or energy giving chase. They weren't about to come back, he was certain. The older man slid from the horse as Fargo dismounted.

"We owe you more than we can pay, mister," he said. "I'm Harry Paxton. This is my niece, Clea."

"Fargo . . . Skye Fargo," the Trailsman said.

"That was mighty good timing and mighty fine shooting, Fargo," Harry Paxton said.

"Why were they out to hang you?" Fargo asked, taking a moment to have a closer look at the young woman. She wasn't tall, her figure neat and tight, her green shirt resting on what seemed to be modest breasts. A small nose was centered on a face of even features, with light brown eyes and firm lips. It was a slightly pugnacious face, he decided, and she had a tomboy quality to her, yet not without a certain sensuality.

"They made a mistake, far as I can figure," Harry Paxton said. "Thought we were somebody else."

"That has to be it," Clea said. "They just came down on us, no explaining, no anything."

Fargo nodded, willing to accept their explanation as he wondered what other paunchy old man and tomboyish girl they could be mistaken for. "You just passing through?" he asked.

"We're on our way to a job," Clea answered. "Uncle Henry's a real good cook and I'm going along to help him."

"Good luck," Fargo said as Henry Paxton went to

the buckboard. Clea came to Fargo, standing very close to him, her light brown eyes grave.

"I hope we can meet up again, Fargo. I'd like to properly thank you for what you did," she said softly.

"Don't think about it. Glad I was there," he said.

"Can't help it. That's the way I am. I don't ever forget good deeds," she said. "Or the bad," she added with a wry smile. Rising onto her toes, she touched her lips to his for a quick, fleeting moment. "I sure won't be forgetting you," she said and hurried back to the buckboard, her tomboy quality accented in the way she stiffly swung her arms and torso, her tight little rear both proper and provocative.

"Thanks again, friend," Harry Paxton called out as they drove away. Clea gazed back thoughtfully but she didn't wave. Fargo stayed, watching the buckboard turn north and finally he rode on, letting the Ovaro move through a shallow stream to cool its ankles. An unusually dense stand of sycamore rose up ahead and Fargo rode into its welcoming shade. The Arizona sycamore, with its long lobes and larger leaves, made a particularly good shade tree. As he rode further into the forest, he saw that the trees dotted the hills on both sides of the forest, and he let the Ovaro walk slowly in the coolness of the shade. The Arizona territory was a place where you welcomed any shade.

Fargo let himself relax, and thought about Clea and her uncle Harry, again wondering who they could have been mistaken for. Their explanation seemed less and less plausible the more he thought about it. A flock of gilded flickers swooped over him, breaking off his thoughts as he enjoyed their beauty. He wanted to reach Yucca Flats but not at the expense of pushing the Ovaro in the midday heat. The imperiousness in Solita Chiltec's note had told him something else. People with her temperament would wait. They expected the world would come to them. All too often, for a great variety of reasons, they were right, Fargo admitted wryly, and continued to ride slowly through the valley of sycamores.

5

The horsemen paused in the thick tree cover of the hills. One, wearing a black kerchief over a dark green shirt, snapped at a tall, thin man on a short-legged yellow dun. "He's a dead man, I tell you. We have him ten to one and we'll come at him from both sides. What the hell are you worried about, dammit?" he said.

"I'm worried about what I've heard about him. He's got eyes like a damn eagle, ears like a whitetail, and he can track like a Comanche," the man on the yellow dun said, his thin face drawn thinner with concern.

"We'll be doing the tracking, not him. As for his damn ears, the woods are full of sounds—buzzing mosquitoes, the crickets, and the stage-horn beetles are noisy as hell. So are squirrels, raccoons, and woodrats. The damn woodpeckers never stop pecking, the crows never shut up, the *chulus* are noisier than the raccoons, and javelinas are always grunting and rooting. Christ, there's plenty of noise to cover us," the one with the black kerchief said. But the thin-faced man still looked worried. "Shit, how do you want to take him?" the other demanded.

"From far away. Long-distance rifle fire. Let him get into the open so there's no chance of him picking us up, then we take him down with rifles," the man said.

"No. Chances are our first shot will miss until we get the range. He'll be off and running, and we might never get another chance," the black-scarfed one said. "We do it my way, keep him between us, slowly moving up on him. When it's the right moment, we charge him. Done and finished, believe me." The other man made no reply but his face made it plain he was still full of misgivings. "Keep moving, stay spread out," the other one ordered.

"Won't work with him. He's not the ordinary rangehand," the thin-faced man grumbled, but moved his horse forward anyway.

The puma does not need to think about the softness of his steps. The hawk sees the prairie chicken miles below him without any strain on his part. The deer need make no effort to feel the branch move a hundred yards away. The reaction and response of all wild creatures are as natural to them as breathing. Only man is without such native, natural ability. Man must develop his abilities, hone his knowledge, perfect his sensitivities. Except, that is, for a few chosen ones, those with special qualities, those who love and admire all that is wild. They are the lucky ones who can approach the perceptiveness of wild creatures. They can absorb the essence of sound, taste, touch, sight, and smell. They can understand the meaning of a bent blade of grass, the message in a puff of wind.

There aren't many—the wild mountain men, the primal Indian scouts, the wilderness hermits, and the Trailsman. As he rode through the sycamore forest, it was one of those innate senses that told Fargo he did not ride alone. With the practice born of experience, he made no move to glance around. Instead, he continued to sit in his saddle casually and let his nostrils flare, drawing in more of the scent that drifted to him. Slowly, he let his olfactory senses paint their own picture. The distinctive odor of horses came first. Not Indian ponies—they had a different smell to them than white men's horses. They were groomed differently, fed differently, carried the smell of different masters. The next scent that came to him was the smell of saddles, leather mixed with horse lather. Lastly, he could faintly make out the scent of wool shirts.

He turned the Ovaro just enough to let himself see up into one hill without obviously turning to look. Now sight took over for smell, that special vision that brought the wisdom of the trail with it. He saw the ends of branches dip, but not in a wavy motion caused by a passing breeze. They bent in a straight line, and Fargo soon caught sight of the riders carefully picking their way through the trees. Again, shifting the Ovaro just enough, he could see the opposite hill without appearing to look. Again, he found the pattern of the branches as they dipped. The riders on the second hill had spread out.

These were no riders moving idly through the hills,

their passage careful and deliberate. They were tailing him, slowly drawing closer. Why? he wondered as he moved the Ovaro forward. The glint of sun on water caught his eye and he shifted direction, soon arriving at an oblong-shaped lake. Now his ears took charge. The two sets of riders had reached the bottom of the hills and had moved out onto the flat ground. But his ears easily distinguished that they stayed in two separate groups. The sound of one group told him that they rode more closely together than the other. He let the Ovaro move toward the lake where the sycamores ended and a dozen black willows grew to the water's edge. He swung the horse into a big, thick willow that hung almost to the ground, forming a fringed curtain. They no doubt saw him move into the willows, he was certain, but there was an open space where the sycamores ended and the willows grew. They'd have to cross it.

Fargo drew the Colt as he waited. His eyes tuned to the trees, and he saw five riders come into view. That left the other five, he grunted to himself. One of the riders wore a black kerchief and moved his horse a few paces forward. "We want to talk," he called out.

"Talk is cheap," Fargo returned from inside the curtain of the willow.

"Talking is better than dying," the man replied.

"Can't argue with that," Fargo returned. "I'm listening."

"I like to see a man when I talk to him," the black-kerchiefed man said.

"I'm naturally shy," Fargo said blandly. Meanwhile,

his eyes once again followed his ears, and soon he saw the second set of five riders sneaking through the sycamore, on their way to circle behind the willows. Noiselessly, Fargo turned in the saddle, holstered the Colt, and drew the big Henry from its rifle case. He leveled the rifle back over the horse's rump while he directed his voice forward. "I'm waiting," he called. "What do you want with me?"

"Our boss wants to talk to you," the man said.

"Why?" Fargo replied as he kept facing the rear, his eyes narrowed through the rifle sights. The five riders came into view, and began to make their way toward the willows. Fargo cast another glance back at the first five. They were staying in place. But they were surely waiting for their friends to take him down with a burst of gunfire from behind, Fargo realized. He was about to return his eyes to the rifle when he spied the small figure walking along the edge of the water a half-dozen yards away. Not more than eight or nine years old, he guessed, she carried a sack of laundry slung over one shoulder, a pail and soap in her other hand.

She'd be walking right into God knows what, Fargo murmured, groaning inside. *Shit*, he cursed silently but he had to swing back to the rifle. The five horsemen were starting to push into the willows, he saw, all with six-guns in their hands, ready to open a barrage of fire. He'd no time left for choosing. His finger pressed the trigger of the rifle, swinging it as he fired. The first rider's gun leaped from his hand as he was blown from his horse. The man beside him flung his arms high into the air as he, too, went down. Fargo fired again and the others went down like ducks in a shooting gallery. All except the fifth one, who swung his horse around and bolted from the trees.

Fargo pushed the Henry into its case and swung back to the five riders in front of him, the Colt in hand again. They were milling about in surprise, aware that their maneuver had gone awry when they spotted the rider who bolted. Fargo started to take aim, but held back as he saw that the little girl was almost in the center of their milling horses, trying to decide which way to run and making only little half starts. If he opened fire, they'd start shooting, furiously and wildly. It was damn near certain she'd take a bullet. His eyes went to the man with the black kerchief, who bent over in the saddle, peering into the willow, expecting the bullets Fargo was poised to fire. As he watched, Fargo saw the crafty expression spread across the man's face. Spinning his horse, he reached down, snatched the little girl up into the saddle with him, and held her in front of him.

"Come out or she gets it," he shouted as the others waited on both sides.

Fargo cursed, and took a moment before he finally answered. "Let her go. She's no part of this," he said.

"She is now," the man said, malicious triumph in his voice. The other four men dropped back a few paces. Fargo's lips drew back in a tight line, his chiseled jaw cast in stone. He had time to wheel and race away, letting the men try to catch him as he bolted from the back of the willows. His eyes fastened on the black-kerchiefed one holding the little girl, at the harsh cruelty he saw in the man's face. There was no compassion, no simple humanity. It was a face that would pull a trigger out of fury and spite. Fargo cursed silently again. The man held the child too tightly, and his horse kept prancing nervously. Fargo saw that he'd not have a shot, not even with his superior marksmanship.

And if he bolted, he'd be playing roulette with the little girl's life. Fargo couldn't bring himself to do that. Slowly, he moved the Ovaro sideways inside the willow, and when he emerged from behind the curtain of fronds he was within six feet of the lake. He halted, the Colt raised, aimed at the black kerchief. "Drop the gun," the man rasped.

"Let her go first. Put her down," Fargo answered.

"And make myself a target? Like hell," the man threw back. Fargo's glance swept the others. They all had a clear shot at him. It'd be only seconds before they took the opportunity, he realized. He had only one move left. It was also the only way to save the child's life. The black-kerchiefed man would toss her aside to get a better shot at him. "The gun, dammit," the man ordered.

Fargo half shrugged and lowered the Colt. He started to bend over in the saddle in what seemed to be a move to toss the gun on the ground alongside the Ovaro. But, using all the power in his thigh muscles, he flung himself sideways out of the saddle. He was diving through the air when he heard the shouts of alarm from behind him. "Shoot, goddammit!" the black-kerchiefed man screamed. He also heard the little girl cry out as she was tossed aside. Then gunfire erupted. Their first shots were too fast and wild, but he had counted on that. He hit the water, feeling the coldness slapping his face as he dove under the surface.

They let go another volley and he tried to dive deeper. The shoreline stayed shallow, not dropping off as he expected it would, and Fargo had to strike out to find deeper water. Dimly, he heard the sound of the horses reach the shoreline, a sound all but drowned out by another volley of shots. Frantically, Fargo tried to reach deeper water, but the shoreline was made up of a long, shallow sandbar that extended far out from the shore. He heard the bullets slam into the water near him as he swam as fast as he could underwater. They had to glimpse him to fire accurately, he knew, and then he felt the bullets hit, the first one grazing his leg, the second his shoulder, the third his ribs. He broke the surface, rolled, and tried to scramble for the shore and the safety of the line of willows.

But the horses were on him in a second, hands grabbing him, pulling him up. Fargo crouched and swung a hard left that connected with somebody's face, and he heard the cry of pain before a half-dozen blows rained down at him. He managed to wrap both arms around a leg, and as he pulled, the figure went down. A gun butt smashed into Fargo's scalp and he felt the blood course down his temple. He was lifted, flung away, and he recognized the voice of the black-kerchiefed man without making out his words. Another shot rang out and Fargo felt his temple burn and sear. He fell backward, hitting the water and sinking below the surface. With his last bit of consciousness, he dimly saw the water turning red around him and then he was floating away. His sight faded, and finally he was wrapped in nothingness. Yet, somehow, he could still wonder whether it was the bullet or drowning that carried him into the void where there was no more wondering, no more feeling, no more of anything.

This was death, then, the abyss, the total absence of time, place, yesterday, tomorrow. With a kind of unconscious consciousness, Fargo felt an awareness. Air, at first. But there is no awareness in death, he thought. No touch of air. Yet there was air—he felt it, and the soft slap of water. It registered only as a strange sensation, not really comprehensible, and even that vanished as quickly as it had come. The void became total once again, the emptiness supreme. He did not feel the hands that cradled his head on the small rise of the sandbar. He was completely unaware of the little girl putting her laundry bag under his head, raising it enough for him to take in air instead of drowning. And of course he didn't know that his attackers, certain he was dead from their bullets, had ridden away.

None of these things did Fargo know, feel, or comprehend in any way, just as he did not feel the other hands that came to drag him out of the lake and onto the shore. He knew nothing about being lifted onto the light, one-horse utility wagon and driven from the lakeside. So when the void lifted again, he felt only a vague sensation, dimly soothing, as if he were being stroked. Slowly, one thing filtered its way to him, beginning to take on a single, all-important meaning: He was alive. That singular, undeniable thought slowly took shape, spreading to envelop him with all its glorious meaning, all its absolute magnitude. He was aware. He was alive. This time there was no void, only sleep, and he gave silent thanks to the difference.

It was the morning of a new day when he woke again. When his eyelids fluttered, finally pulling open, he first felt his nakedness, then the pain in his still-throbbing body. The smoothness of a sheet beneath him drifted into his consciousness and he forced his eyes to open wider. He began to distinguish light and darkness. Forcing himself to focus his eyes, the headboard of a bed took shape, then, beyond, log walls, and finally a low-roofed room. Memory rushed over him in a sudden burst and he saw himself diving into the lake, being attacked, and the stinging pain of the bullets as they struck. He saw and almost felt the blood erupting, coursing down over his face, obliterating his vision.

As suddenly as they had flashed before him, the memories snapped off. He moved gingerly, and brought his hand to his face. There was no caked blood and he felt the touch of ointment on his face, his shoulders, his chest. He moved, trying to turn over and heard the cry of pain that must have come from him. He lay still, his body suddenly on fire in a half-dozen places. He heard footsteps hurrying toward him. Trying desperately to focus again, Fargo saw a woman appear, halting alongside the bed where he lay. "You've come around. I was getting worried," she said. "Thought maybe the bullet that hit your temple might have gone a lot deeper. Welcome back to the world."

"Always wondered what an angel would look like," Fargo said, taking in her wide, pleasant face, her brown hair pulled back in a bun, brown eyes, a sweet mouth—a face with a kind of rawboned attractiveness to it. A loose, one-piece brown muslin dress hung on her ample figure, wide-hipped and deep-breasted.

She smiled and her stark quality softened. "No angel," the woman said. "I'm Bess Robinson. It was my little girl, Susie, that they grabbed. She told me you could have run but you gave yourself up to save her. I figured that needed repaying. So did Susie."

"How do you mean that?" Fargo queried.

"She ran away and hid, and watched them shoot bullets into you while you were trying to get away in the lake. She watched them ride away and leave you for dead. But she wanted to see for herself. Susie's always been that way. Doubting Thomas, she is. She went out into the lake and found you laying on top of a small rise on a sandbar. By putting her laundry bag under your head, she lifted your mouth and nose out of the water high enough for you to take in air instead of water. Then she ran back here and told me what had happened. I went to the lake with her and we dragged you out, then brought you here. Brought your horse, too. He's in my barn out back."

"Two angels, not one," Fargo murmured. "Where's Susie now?"

"Visiting a friend. She'll be back later," Bess Robinson said and a small smile slid across her face. "So, Mr. Skye Fargo, why were they so anxious to kill you?" she asked. "Found your name in with your clothes when I took them off you."

"That's something I'd like to know, too," Fargo said, hissing in pain as he tried to move.

"You need more ointment," the woman said, and took a stoppered bottle from a shelf and began to rub the soothing salve over his body. "Comfrey, pennyroyal, and yarrow. Wonderful for cuts and bruises." She massaged the salve in with long, smooth strokes, covering every part of his body.

"I'm not sure I need it all over," he said evenly.

"Some places I rub in are for you. Others are for me," the woman said.

"That's being honest," Fargo remarked.

"I'm long past playing coy games," Bess Robinson said as she continued to rub salve across his groin. "Haven't had my way with a man's body for a long time and never with one such as yours. I'm making the most of it." She let a tiny giggle escape her lips. "Let's say I want you to recover . . . for the both of us."

"I'll go with that," Fargo murmured. "What are you and a little girl doing out here on your own, Bess?"

"We were left by a man, going on eight years now. He was always going out chasing wild dreams and schemes. I heard he was killed somewhere a few years back. Powell Lake, where you almost had your last swim, has a real fine stock of rainbow trout, pink salmon, pickerel, and largemouth bass. People come fishing but they mostly don't have the right bait or the right gear. I make a living selling them both."

She moved up to spread the salve on his chest and he had the chance to study her more closely. Her somewhat hard face could soften easily, he saw, but it never lost its strength. Her large-boned body was matched by an inner resourcefulness, he decided, a strength that had its own kind of admirable appeal. When the little girl's voice sounded from outside, Bess tossed a sheet over his groin. "Just being proper. Susie's old beyond her years. She's seen about everything," Bess Robinson said as her daughter burst into the room like a ray of sunshine.

"You're awake, Fargo!" Susie said excitedly, and turned to her mother. "I told you he'd come around."

"Thanks for everything you did, Susie," Fargo said. "Anything I can do is yours, honey."

"There's one thing," Susie said. "I want to ride your Ovaro. I've never seen a horse beautiful as that."

"Susie's a good rider," Bess put in.

"Just go ride him. He's a real smart horse. He'll be good with you. He'll know who's on him," Fargo said.

Susie squealed with gleeful excitement. "First start peeling some potatoes," her mother said and the little girl hurried from the room. "Ready to sleep?" Bess asked Fargo and he nodded, suddenly aware of how fatigued he felt. His body throbbed, especially where the bullets had creased him.

"I sure am. Guess I'm not ready for too much yet," Fargo said.

"Not yet. But salve and sleep will do what they're supposed to do," Bess said and Fargo let his eyes close, falling into sleep at once. He woke late in the night when Bess came in to rub more salve over his body. It became a pattern in the days that followed, and each day Fargo felt himself growing stronger, the throbbing ebbing from his body. Finally, the day came when he could stand and put on his trousers without groaning with pain. He had spent an increasing amount of his resting time thinking about the attack that had nearly cost him his life. He had been their target, and he wanted to know why. He could find no reason, not even a clue for the assault. But he'd try, he decided. Perhaps he could find something. He'd have a try at it before he went on, he decided.

While he recovered, Susie rode the Ovaro every day and Fargo enjoyed her happiness. But finally, as a silent night grew long, he lay awake as Bess Robinson came to the side of his bed. "You're well as I can make you. I suppose you'll be leaving," she said in a sad tone.

He nodded. "Got places to be, things to do," he said, noticing that she wore the same one-piece, loose muslin garment she had on when he first saw her. "I'm beholden to you, Bess," he said.

"No need, not after what you did for Susie," she

said. "I'm going to miss rubbing your body every day. Been thinking there ought to be one last time."

Fargo smiled back. "Sounds like a right good idea," he agreed. Bess brought herself closer, bent over and began to rub her hands down his chest, her ample figure brushing at him as she did. She moved downward, her hands moving to his waist, rubbing there slowly before moving on to his abdomen, then his hips. He reached out and stopped her and she frowned at him. "You're always the one dressed. Seems it ought to be different this time," he said.

"So it does," she murmured, a little smile alighting on her lips. She raised both arms at once, whisked the dress up over her head, and tossed it aside with one motion. Bringing her arms down, she waited for him to take in her large breasts that hung heavily on her chest. Very red nipples rose from the center of each, set onto reddish brown areolas. A slightly thick yet very earthy waistline wrapped below a chunky abdomen, her loose triangle, more unruly than dense, spread wide over a pronounced pubic mound. Her thighs were muscular, with the appeal of power and firmness.

She reached out again, running her hands down his lower torso, resting on his groin as he felt his own response to her touch. He heard the deepness of her breath as he grew firm for her and she found the prize she wanted, her fingers curling around him. No gentle massage, now, no delicacy of touch. Instead, he felt her eagerness, the desire that welled up through her fingers as she pumped, caressed, and clasped, little murmuring sounds escaping from her lips: "Ah, ah, yes ... ah yes, oh, Jeez, oh my God." Bess Robinson brought herself down over him, and began to rub herself up and down his body, pressing her full, wide breasts against his abdomen, chest, and face, her dark red nipples seeking his mouth, finding the pleasure she wanted with a cry of triumphal delight.

She sank down on his shaft, enveloping him, taking him fully into her dark, warm portal and her cries rose in deep, dark, almost animalistic sounds. She made love not so much with frenzy but with an almost savagery that had to come from too many unfulfilled yesterdays and unpromised tomorrows. Her hands dug into him as she engulfed him with every urging her body could bring, turning, twisting, surging, thrusting. "God, ah, ah, ah ... ah, my God, ah, aaagggh," she groaned and cried, and he found himself rising to match the driving urgings of her body. Finally, when the moment came to her, Bess Robinson buried her face into his chest as she cried out, a guttural, rapturous cry from somewhere deep within her. He felt her entire body buck against him in a series of convulsive shudders that only stopped when it seemed there was no more gasping or groaning left inside her. She lay with him, her belly still shuddering against him, tiny afterthoughts of her climax.

He held her when she finally lay still and she slept against him, her large frame seeming slighter than it was, as if it had been drained of all its normal strength. When morning came, she awoke early, taking a moment more to clasp herself to him. "Anytime you want to come back, Fargo," she said, her wide mouth growing wider with a meaningful smile. She brushed her hair back with one hand, a suddenly very girlish motion.

"You look younger," he told her honestly.

"I feel younger," she said, then rose and pulled her dress on. He said good-bye soon after, with Susie there, stroking the Ovaro for a last time.

"Bring him back," she pleaded.

"Might just do that," Fargo said, hugging her little form and swinging into the saddle. Mother and daughter waved as he rode away. They had been the only good thing that had happened since he left Julie, he reflected. Clea Paxton and her uncle had been a good deed but not a good thing, unanswered questions still haunting them. Fargo turned the Ovaro toward the lake, his jaw tightening as he did. It was noon when he reached the water, a quiet, serene spot now, and his eyes swept the shoreline. Over a week had passed and the lake had received some visitors, he quickly saw, but there were only a few prints—a few single horses, and the tracks of one other wagon besides Bess Robinson's.

Fargo's eyes stayed narrowed as he moved back and forth along the land leading from the shoreline. The tracks he was certain he would find finally appeared alongside the edge of the sycamores—the trail of five horses bunched together. First there were the deep prints of horses at a gallop, which grew shallower as they slowed. He allowed a grunt of satisfaction as he followed the tracks south across a dry arroyo where the creosote bushes grew thick, and finally to a ramshackle town on the edge of nowhere. Buildings appeared in front of him and as the last of the day waned, he rode through the typical single main street. The town was made of frame structures, which badly needed paint and polish. A number of pack mules lined the street, along with a dozen or so wagons, mostly one-horse huckster wagons and rugged farm wagons. Prospecting and farming hardscrabble land was obviously the main business in the area.

But he saw a good-sized supply store that told him there was a trade in travelers passing through the region. The tracks he had been following disappeared in the hoofprints of the main street. But they had led him here, close enough to the doorway of the saloon only a few dozen yards away. He paused in front of the place and saw that it bore the town's name: Red Dust Saloon. Well named, Fargo grunted as night descended, and he guided the Ovaro to the back of the saloon, where he hitched the horse to a post out of sight of the tavern's entrance. Returning to the front, he went inside and found a larger crowd than he'd expected. The large room was cleaner than he'd expected as well, the sawdust on the floor fresh, the tables with real cloth on them.

A half-dozen girls in satiny dresses lounged against the far wall, but Fargo sauntered right to the bar. A short but powerfully built barkeep came up to him at once. "Something to wet your whistle, stranger?" he asked.

"Bourbon," Fargo replied. "Came in looking for somebody. Don't know his name but I was told he comes in here. Wears a black kerchief, usually has some friends with him."

"What might you want with him?" the bartender said, instantly anxious to avoid trouble before it started. Fargo smiled inwardly at the man's experienced caution.

"Got some range work. He was recommended to me," Fargo said blandly.

"Sounds like Willie Drayton. Don't know anybody else who wears a black kerchief," the bartender said as he poured the bourbon.

"He come in here every night?" Fargo asked, keeping his tone casual.

"Not every night but often enough, maybe four times a week," the barkeep said.

"I'll wait a spell, have a sandwich while I do," Fargo said.

"I've got venison. It's a lot better than that tough longhorn beef," the man said.

"Venison's fine," Fargo said, taking his drink to a small table in the corner, hidden away yet affording him a good view of the door. He sat down and immediately began to think about how to avoid a wild shootout when Willie Drayton and company came in. He wanted at least one of them alive and able to answer questions. One of the girls brought his sandwich and he ate slowly as he wrestled with his thoughts, finding none that gave him any sense of comfort. The night grew long and Drayton didn't enter the saloon.

Fargo found himself not entirely unhappy. He still hadn't come up with a plan that satisfied him, and he finally rose when the last of the customers began to drift to the door. "Guess they won't be dropping by tonight," he remarked to the barkeep. "I'll stop by tomorrow night."

"They hang out due west of town, past Papago Creek. Sam Hyssop rents them an old house for a dollar a month," the man volunteered. Fargo forced himself to keep the excitement from exploding across his face.

"Much obliged," he said and walked from the bar with a wave good night. He retrieved the Ovaro and rode from town, turning the horse west as the moon hung far beyond the midnight sky. The pale orb was moving toward the horizon when he finally found the creek, riding through it and pressing on. The house, a large, low-roofed building, just came into sight as the moon slid below the earth, turning the night into inky blackness. Fargo saw a wide, low-branched paloverde and guided the horse toward it. He dismounted and lay down. Closing his eyes, he fell asleep in moments, unwilling to explore the house in pitch darkness. He had managed almost two hours' sleep before the dawn's sun woke him and he sat up, blinking his eyes clear.

In the morning light, the house revealed itself in all of its paint-peeling shabbiness. An equally decrepit barn stood alongside it, the sounds of horses emanating from inside. Fargo let his eyes sweep the land surrounding the house, most of it open range. But he saw one long, large stretch of brittlebush that extended from one side of the paloverde to the house and beyond. He rose and began to edge toward the foliage when the door of the house opened and a figure emerged, carrying a bucket. Fargo froze in place under the low branches of the paloverde and instantly recognized the man as one of those who had pumped bullets at him as he tried to flee in the lake. He had found the right house, Fargo told himself with grim satisfaction. The man filled the bucket at a well then went back into the house. It was but a few minutes later that Fargo smelled the strong scent of coffee brewing. Surprising them at breakfast seemed as good a chance as he'd get, Fargo decided and dropped to his stomach.

Carefully, he began to crawl through the foliage. The brittlebush was a favorite of the Apache and the Comanche as they stole up on a settler's home. The yellow-gray bushes were tall enough to afford protective cover. Perhaps equally important to the Indian, brittlebush was tough and sinuous, able to stand almost without moving as one crawled through it. A settler glancing out his window would be unlikely to see the foliage move as a hundred other plants would. The smell of coffee grew stronger as Fargo reached the house and, pulling himself up, he carefully peeked through a window. Four of the men sat around a roughly hewn log table. The fifth one was pouring from a chipped tin coffeepot.

All wore trousers and undershirts, their guns hanging on the backs of their chairs. One had a black kerchief hanging from his rear pocket and Fargo took a moment to linger on the man's cruel face. The others conversed in monosyllables as they dipped black bread into their coffee. Fargo rose, moving forward on footsteps silent as those of a cougar on the prowl. He reached the door and sent it flying open with one hard kick. The five figures whirled, their surprise turning to dumbfounded astonishment, their faces mirroring disbelief, shock, and fear. "Having breakfast with a dead man bother you boys?" Fargo asked. They just stared back, jaws hanging open. One licked his suddenly dry lips and his twitching hand made a movement toward the gun on the chair. "Don't even try. You can't kill a ghost," Fargo said.

The man's hand stopped moving, but didn't stop twitching. "Jesus," he rasped. Fargo's eyes cut to Willie Drayton. The man stood with the coffeepot in midair, frozen in place.

"Move away from the table, all of you," Fargo said.

"You're dead, goddammit. You're dead," Willie Drayton muttered.

"That's right," Fargo said. "And so will you be if you don't move away from the table." His eyes flicked across the others, seeing them still gaping at him in disbelief and near-panic. Willie Drayton stayed glued in place and then, with surprising suddenness, exploded into action, flinging the coffeepot. Fargo saw the lid fall open as the pot hurtled at him, the boiling stream of coffee about to hit him in the face. He twisted away but he still felt the painful shower of scalding coffee. Cursing from the sharp pain, he swung back in time to see Willie Drayton grabbing his gun from the back of his chair.

The man started to turn to fire as the Colt barked and two shots slammed into Willie Drayton. His chest flew open in a shower of red that sprayed in all directions. Even the black kerchief hanging from his pocket was suddenly soaked. As Drayton collapsed, Fargo swung the Colt, seeing two of the others diving for their guns. He fired and both men shuddered, their hands still outstretched trying to reach the chairs as they fell to the floor. Fargo flung himself to the floor behind the table as three shots whizzed past him, the last two men having reached their guns. Flattened on the floor, he fired under the table at the four legs in his sights. One pair of legs buckled and the man cursed in pain as he went down. But he still tried to fire his gun, and Fargo let the Colt bark again. The man's groan of pain broke off as he clasped both hands to his belly and rolled on the floor.

Fargo rose, seeing the last figure running from the house. He followed, reloading as he did. The man, still in his undershirt, had reached the barn, and Fargo paused in the doorway as he called out. "Don't try it. Come out with your hands up!" he shouted. There was no answer and Fargo stepped outside, the Colt raised. "Don't be a damned fool. I'll nail you before you even have a chance. Come out with your hands up." Fargo called again, and once more there was no answer. Then suddenly he heard the splintering of wood. The picture formed itself instantly. The man had thrown a saddle on his horse and now he was kicking out the dry, weather-weakened boards at the rear of the barn, making an exit for himself. With another crash of splintering wood, Fargo heard the hoofbeats of a horse racing out of the rear of the barn.

"Shit," Fargo swore as he skirted the barn and ran toward the paloverde where he had left the Ovaro. He caught a glimpse of the fleeing rider, atop a very ordinary brown quarter horse. It would be no match for the Ovaro, Fargo knew as he reached the paloverde and leaped into the saddle. He raced from underneath the tree, seeing the horseman galloping across open, dry, flatland. Fargo put the Ovaro's muscled body into a smooth stride and quickly closed in on the outlaw. The man turned in the saddle and fired two wild shots at him before turning back to keep his horse running all out. When the man fired off another wild shot, Fargo slowed the Ovaro. He was certain the man would be reloading and firing more, and Fargo decided against risking a lucky bullet. He hung back, letting the Ovaro follow the man at a steady pace.

It didn't take long before Fargo saw the man's horse tire, its stride begin to shorten. Fargo held his pace as the distance grew ever shorter between him and his quarry. The man glanced back and Fargo saw panic come into his face as he whipped at his horse, but the animal only slowed further. Fargo reached back, drew the rifle from its saddle case, and brought it to his shoulder. He wanted the man alive and able to talk. That meant a careful, well-aimed shot. He waited, ready as the man turned in the saddle again, bringing his six-gun up to fire. Fargo, the rifle already aimed, pressed the trigger, and saw the man clutch at his shoulder as he cursed in pain.

He pulled on his horse's reins to keep his seat in the saddle as Fargo fired again, at the same shoulder. The man flew sideways from his horse, hit the ground hard, and lay still. Fargo rode up to him, and seeing the six-gun on the ground, he kicked the gun aside. The man turned, clutching one hand to his shattered shoulder. "Son of a bitch," he growled. "You're supposed to be dead."

"Things just don't always turn out right," Fargo said. "But they'll get a lot worse unless I get some answers. Why me?"

The man glared up at him as he clearly understood the question. "I don't know," he said.

Fargo pulled the hammer back on the Colt. "I've got a short fuse," he said.

"Willie Drayton hired us. He's the only one who knew anything. All he told us was that we were going to take you out. Paid real good money, three hundred each. Nobody asked questions."

"Willie Drayton was a small-time gun hand. He never had that kind of money. Somebody hired him. Who?" Fargo pressed.

"He used a name a couple of times . . . Arriaga . . . a Mexican. Jesus, that's all I know, I swear it," the man said. Fargo decided to believe him. The pain and fear in the man's face left him no room to lie.

"Go on, ride," Fargo said and holstered the Colt.

"Help me. I'm losing a lot of blood," the man said.

"You tried to kill me. You're lucky I'm letting you ride away," Fargo said.

"What if there's no doc in Red Dust?" the man whined.

"Go to the bar or the blacksmith. I don't much care. Now ride before I change my mind," Fargo said, and waited as the man went to his horse, using his good arm to pull himself into the saddle. When he had ridden out of sight, Fargo swung onto the Ovaro and turned east. He hoped to get to Yucca Flats without any more interruptions.

6

The sun was moving across the late afternoon sky when Fargo reached Yucca Flats. It was a small but neat, orderly town flanked by giant saguaro cactus. He rode through the town's avenues until he found Cactus Lane. Just as Solita Chiltec's note said, there was but one house on the street. A gray-haired, affable woman with a large apron tied around her midsection answered his knock. "Come to see Solita Chiltec," Fargo said.

The woman made a sympathetic noise with her lips. "I'm afraid you're almost two days late," she said. "Solita's left. She went off with the man she's been waiting for."

Fargo felt the frown instantly dig into his forehead. "The man she's been waiting for?" he echoed.

"Yes. She was getting ready to leave without him when he finally arrived," the woman said.

The crease deepened on his brow. "You catch his name?" Fargo asked.

"Yes. Skye Fargo. Solita mentioned it often while she was waiting here," the woman said.

Fargo's mouth tightened as a combination of astonishment and alarm swept through him. Something he didn't understand was going on, but he didn't have time to think it through. He was swept by only one certainty, and it spelled trouble. "You know which way they went?" he asked.

"Solita had hired a lot of people. She was going to a place where they were all to meet, just outside of Lookout Rock. You take the road northeast and you'll come to it," the woman said.

"Much obliged," Fargo said and put the pinto into a fast canter. Solita Chiltec was in trouble. He didn't know why or how—the only question was whether he was going to be too late to help her. He reached the road that curved northeast and kept the pinto at a steady, ground-eating canter, moving through land covered with lupine, brittlebush, mesquite, and acacias. Luckily, the road was not heavily traveled and just before the day closed down he spotted the tracks of two horses riding together. Dismounting, he ran his fingers over the hoofprints, and found they were not more than one or two days old. Confident he had found the tracks he sought, Fargo followed, keeping on the road until night fell. He then halted at a stand of serviceberry and slept until dawn.

He followed the prints again with the new day, finally pausing where the prints stopped beside a shallow creek. Again, his fingers examined the tracks, and found they were still firm, not more than a few hours old. Grunting in satisfaction, he hurried the pinto on, and when a line of pedestal rocks rose up alongside the road he swung toward them. Riding through various rock formations, he stayed parallel to the road below and enjoyed the bright flashes of one turpentine bush after another as they appeared, always unexpectedly, amid the barren rocks. It was midafternoon when he finally saw the two riders on the road below.

One, he instantly saw, rode a pinto, the horse's color a glossy black and white, but an otherwise poorly marked specimen with weak hindquarters and a narrow front, hardly deserving of the name Ovaro. Fargo moved his horse a little closer, where he could get a better look at the riders. The man wore a gray shirt and Fargo picked out his lean face with a long jaw, his black hair slicked down. When the man glanced around, Fargo saw a thin, tight mouth, and a face with more hardness than strength in it. Squinting, Fargo saw that he wore an army Josylen revolver; a single-action, five-shot piece with a tendency to shoot slow.

Fargo's eyes went to the woman beside him, seeing her straight nose and finely chiseled lips. Her luxurious, jet black hair was pulled back and fell down across her shoulder blades. Fargo's eyes went back to her face and noted the high-cheekboned regal beauty of it that also carried a steely arrogance heightened by slight black eyebrows that seemed permanently fixed in an arch. From where he observed, her skin seemed to have an unusual coppery tint to it, but he wondered if that was just the sun bouncing off the sandstone rocks. He dropped back again and began to make his way down from the rocks, holding the Ovaro to careful, almost silent steps.

Staying in the low line of rocks, he drew close enough to hear their voices. "We ought to reach Lookout Rock in another hour or so," the young woman said, and Fargo could now see that she had a long, lithe body, narrow-hipped and elegantly proportioned, a body both sinuous and sensuous under her white shirt and loose-fitting riding britches. He saw a small *tinaja* come into sight, one of the natural water wells that dotted the southwest, made of rock and filled with rainwater. "Let's water the horses," she said and the man followed her to the *tinaja* and dismounted with her. Solita Chiltec stepped back as her horse drank, and the man suddenly came up behind her.

"End of the line, honey," he said.

Solita turned to him, a furrow creasing her high, smooth forehead. "I beg your pardon?" she said.

"End of the line for you," the man repeated and Solita Chiltec stared at him, fury turning the furrow into a frown.

"What is this? What are you saying?" she demanded.

"I was waiting for a better spot but this'll have to do," the man said. "But before you go, you get to have a last screw."

Fargo had heard enough. He moved the Ovaro out of the rocks, emerging from a narrow passage and once again pulled the rifle from its saddle case. He needed the long-range accuracy of the big Henry. Nor could he get closer without being heard, and he didn't want to risk what that might bring. He was starting to bring the rifle to his shoulder when he saw the man sink an underhand blow into Solita's stomach. She gasped in pain, her willowy figure doubling up as she fell forward to her knees. He was on her at once, throwing her onto her back and falling atop her, starting to pull her loose riding britches down.

"No! Stop, damn you!" he heard the young woman cry, seeing her rake one hand across his cheek.

"Goddamn bitch," he swore and smashed a fist into Solita Chiltec's face. She used one arm to partly deflect the blow but still caught the brunt of it on the chin. Pinning her arm down, he pulled at her clothes as Solita fought, wriggling and shifting against him. But now he presented one clean shot, and Fargo took aim and fired at the man's upraised ass. The man cried out in pain as the bullet plowed into his left buttock. "Ow, Jesus!" he roared as he fell from on top of Solita, landing on his side. He yanked his gun out and swivelled frantically about to find a target. By the time he zeroed in on the distant horseman, Fargo's second shot exploded.

It shattered the man's kneecap and he screamed again, clutching at his leg and falling onto his back. Fargo had the Ovaro charge toward the two figures when he saw Solita pull herself free. She whirled and pulled the little pistol from inside the waistband of her shirt, an American arms rimfire derringer, Fargo saw. "No!" he shouted but he was too late as she pumped two bullets into the figure at her feet.

"Stinking, rotten pig!" she shouted but the man only shuddered and lay still. Fargo reined to a halt and leaped from the saddle as Solita Chiltec turned to him. He saw her eyes look over the Ovaro first, then slowly move toward him. Her finely etched lips fell open, her dark brown eyes grew wide in a combination of relief and dismay. "My God . . . oh, my God. *You're* Skye Fargo," she breathed.

"Go to the head of the class," he said and glanced down at the figure on the ground. "And now we'll never know who he is," Fargo added.

"No, I guess not," she said, tucking the derringer inside her waistband. "I just didn't want him coming at me again. I saw my chance and took it." Fargo's eyes moved across her face, down to the V of the white shirt that showed off her delicate collarbone. What he had thought a coppery tone from a distance turned out to be something even more unusual—she had a golden glow, almost as if little flecks of gold were mixed in with the pale tan of her skin. She stepped closer, her dark eyes searching his face. "Thank God you were here," she said.

"Better late than never, I guess," Fargo said blandly, putting away the rifle.

"I had just about given up hearing from you when he came," she said with a contemptuous glance at the still figure.

"He told you he was me," Fargo said and she nodded.

"I believed him. I knew you rode an Ovaro. Actually, I was a little surprised at how shabby a horse it was but I was so anxious to believe you had arrived that I didn't dwell on it," she said. "Shall I introduce myself formally? I've papers in my bag to prove who I am."

"No need. Besides, you sound like your notes," he said.

"Meaning what, exactly?" she returned, her finely etched lips finally breaking into a smile.

"Brisk. In control. A touch of arrogance. It's in your face, too, along with the beauty," he said.

"If I'd any doubts whether you're the real Skye Fargo, I don't now," she said. "You fit everything I've heard about you," Solita said.

"But you've questions to answer," Fargo said.

"Of course, but not here," she said with a distastefull glance at the figure on the ground. She swung onto her horse with a smooth, graceful motion that made her breasts sway in beautiful unison. He climbed onto the Ovaro and came up beside her.

"I know the men I sent to get you did very poorly, but you didn't even answer my second note. What made you finally decide to come?"

"Unexpected things," he said, knowing it was a weak answer. But she accepted it and he liked that. It showed she could temper her arrogance with wisdom.

"You want to know why I sent for you, what I want of you?" Solita asked.

"There's more I want to know but we'll start with that," Fargo answered

"I'm going to follow a trail, a very special trail, but I'll need you to help me. I've a lot of information that can be useful—old writings, some maps, miscellaneous rumors, a whole bagful of things. But I need someone who will see what I won't see, read the signs I can't read, interpret the things I can't," Solita said.

"What kind of a trail are you talking about?" Fargo asked.

"The trail of Francisco Vasquez de Coronado," she said.

A frown dug into Fargo's brow, and he turned her words over in his mind as a sense of disbelief crept through him. "The Spanish conquistador Coronado?"

"Exactly," Solita said, her chin lifting with a touch of defiance.

"Let's try this on again. You want me to find a trail that's three hundred and fifty years old?" he said, and her nod was coolly regal. "You're kidding, I hope," he said.

"I'm completely serious," she said.

"You're plumb crazy," he returned.

"No," she said. "I've a very large grant from a university to follow Coronado's trail, to stop at every place he did, to catalog the land, the trees, plants, flowers, and animals, and find out how much things are the same and how much they are different. It'll be a fascinating project."

"It'll be an impossible project," he said.

"No, not with the material I have and with you beside me," she said. "Coronado had two purposes when he went north from Mexico: One was to find more gold to bring back to Spain. The other was to follow a band of Aztec warriors who had run off with sacred Aztec objects. I want to find out if he captured any of these sacred objects as well as anything else he did. I've hired a lot of people to do the things I'll want done at every important place along the way. I was on my way to meet with them when that swine attacked me."

"That's one of the things that needs explaining," Fargo said. "That took planning. How'd he know you were waiting for me?"

She thought for a moment. "It was no secret that I'd sent for you. I'd told a number of people I wanted to hire the very best. Passing himself off as you was a clever way to get to me and the money he expected I'd be carrying."

"You think he was just after the money?" Fargo asked.

"Absolutely," she said.

Fargo thought over her answer. It couldn't be simply rejected, yet it didn't satisfy him completely. "Ten gunhands tried to kill me so I wouldn't get to you. You don't see any connection?"

She paused in thought once more. "No, except that it could have been more of the same. They also expected I'd be carrying a lot of money. It'd be harder for them if you were with me. They tried to make sure you weren't."

"Both of them just after the money, huh?" Fargo said.

"Yes," Solita replied.

Fargo held back further questions, but knew he was still far from satisfied. Perhaps her answers were simply reasonable to her, even logical. Or perhaps she didn't want to search any further. But he was never big on coincidences, and the two attacks were too convenient for him. Still, he had no better explanation and he decided to withhold judgment. Her words broke into his thoughts to trigger something else he wanted resolved.

"I wrote that I'd be making a lucrative offer," she said. "A thousand dollars. Now, you have to admit that's a lot more than the usual rate," Solita said.

"No argument there," Fargo agreed as Julie leaped into his thoughts. Julie and the promise he'd made to her was why he had come in the first place. He'd push aside doubts and unresolved questions for that promise. Fargo noted Solita was studying him as the thoughts ran through his mind. But there was no apprehensiveness in her face, no pleading in her big, dark eyes, only a haughty certainty. And something else, he noted. A kind of quiet amusement, as if she were merely waiting for something certain to happen.

"You've a deal," he said. "But then you never doubted that, did you?" Her little grin was an enigmatic answer. Solita Chiltec was a fascinating young woman, Fargo decided, a patrician hauteur that encased a throbbing sensuality. "I've a condition," he said and she waited to hear it. "I want my fee in a bank draft up front, sent to a Julie Neemeyer in Temple Rock, Colorado territory," he said.

Her thin, black eyebrows arched a fraction higher. "A very special woman?" she said.

"A very special friend who happens to be a woman," Fargo answered.

Solita's lips pursed and the cool amusement came

back into her eyes again as she peered at him. "A man of many dimensions," she remarked.

"I've a feeling you beat me at that," he said. The little enigmatic smile touched her lips again as she put her horse forward into a trot.

"I'll send the draft soon as we reach Lookout," she said and he hurried the Ovaro to draw up beside her. He enjoyed watching her grace as she rode, her body moving as one with her mount. Her breasts swayed in a smooth rhythm that added to her striking suppleness. Her long waist dipped and straightened and her legs showed their lean tautness under the riding britches.

"How did a beautiful woman such as you happen to get interested in Coronado and his trail?" he asked.

"Is there some reason a beautiful woman can't be interested in things like that?" she returned.

"No, but most aren't," Fargo said.

"That's the world's fault, not theirs," Solita said crisply.

"Maybe so." He laughed and then his eyes narrowed at her as he realized something. "You didn't answer the question," he said. "I think it's a technique you perfected. You deflect questions and people think they've been answered."

"Obviously it doesn't work with everyone." Solita smiled. "I studied Aztec history, got interested in that period and especially in Coronado's trail. I applied for a grant and it was accepted." It was a smooth answer though hardly detailed, Fargo noted.

Soon after, they passed a tall rock that rose in a series of steps as a lookout perch, and he found himself riding into a sizeable town that boasted a church, a wheelwright, and a bank. He waited outside while Solita went into the bank, then returned with the bank draft in an envelope made out to Julie. "We'll drop it off at the depot. It'll go out with tomorrow's stage," Solita said.

"Good enough," Fargo said and rode through town beside her, noticing a wagon dealer with a big lot full of assorted rigs.

"My people will be waiting just east of town," Solita said as she led the way. Dusk had begun to gather when they left town and Fargo saw the riders and wagons already assembled in a loose half circle. He dismounted with Solita as she greeted a man who hurried to meet her, a medium-built man with a short mustache and a strong face. "Matt Benton," she introduced.

"Heard of you, Fargo. Bet you've never had this kind of trail to read," Benton said with a firm handshake.

"Never," Fargo said.

"Matt's my trail foreman. He'll be in charge of the diggers, the guards, the wagon drivers, everyone. Except you, of course," Solita said as the man strode off with a wave.

"Diggers, guards, wagon drivers?" Fargo frowned at Solita.

"I wanted the right people for the right jobs. I don't know what I'll be finding. I wanted drivers who know how to drive with care in any kind of terrain, guards who know how to shoot, diggers with experience in careful excavating," Solita explained. He nodded, impressed with the amount of preliminary planning she had put into her project. "I've so much to go over with you but it'll have to wait till morning, I'm afraid," she said. Fargo nodded as he followed her glance at the night slowly rolling over the land. She touched his arm, an ever-so-light yet authoritative touch, before hurrying her way into the circle of wagons.

"This is a surprise," the voice said behind him and he turned to see the tomboy figure with the open, fresh face.

"I'll be damned," he said. "You alone?"

"No, Uncle Harry's with me. Come on," she invited, her hand closing around his as she led him away. He caught Solita watching him walk hand in hand with Clea and thought he detected a chilly interest slide over her elegant face. He went with Clea to a spot near the center of the circle of wagons where Harry Paxton emerged from behind a fully stocked chuck wagon, replete with a possum belly, squirrel can, wreck pan, and Dutch ovens. "Look who I found," Clea announced.

"Damn, this sure is a surprise." Harry Paxton grinned.

"To me, too," Fargo said. "You said you were on your way to a job. This is it, I take it."

"That's right," Harry Paxton said as questions kept flashing through Fargo's mind.

"No mistake, then," he said.

"About what?" Harry frowned.

"About those men mistaking you for somebody else that day," Fargo said. "Wondered about it then, and I'm sure of it now."

"Then why were they so anxious to hang Harry and me?" Clea asked.

"To stop him from joining Solita. Without a cook, there'd be no expedition. Maybe permanently, maybe just long enough to let them do more," Fargo said.

"You just putting out wild ideas?" Clea asked suspiciously.

"It fits with other things," he said.

"Well, we're here, thanks to you, and that's all I care about. Now I've some supper to get ready," Harry said as he turned away. Clea's arm found Fargo's as she walked from the wagons with him.

"I'm glad you're here," she said. "This whole idea seems so crazy, but maybe you can make it work."

"That's a damn big maybe," Fargo replied.

"It's not the only reason I'm glad you're here. I haven't stopped thinking about you that afternoon. I've been hoping we'd meet again somehow and here you are. It's like it was planned to happen," she said.

"Not everything planned works out," he told her.

"I'm good at finding ways to make things work," Clea said and withdrew her arm. "Now, I've got to go help Harry." She hurried off, her small figure swaggering off, her little rear end round and tight. He led the Ovaro away, and found a spot to unsaddle the horse and let him eat some oats. It grew dark, the only light cast by the cooking fires, and he sat down and sampled an omelette of Harry's, finding it tasty. He had just finished when Solita approached.

"Wanted to go over your equipment but it'll have to wait till day," he told her.

"You'll find it in order," Solita said and folded her long figure down beside him. He decided she couldn't make a movement that wasn't graceful. "How come you and my assistant cook got so friendly so quickly?" she slid at him almost casually.

"We met before. Some unfriendly gents were going to hang her and her uncle," Fargo said and saw Solita's eyebrows arch higher than usual. "It adds to what I'm thinking," he said.

"Which is what?"

"That somebody is out to get to you and not just for whatever money you might be carrying," Fargo said.

"Do you have any ideas as to who? I certainly don't," Solita said.

"Can't come up with anyone but I haven't given it a lot of thought yet," he said. "I'll let you know if I do."

"Please," she said. "But I want your concentration on reading trail marks, not on fanciful schemes." He heard the edge of imperiousness edge her tone.

"How'd you come to hire Harry Paxton and Clea?" he asked.

"I didn't. I hired a man named Vittorio. He came down with a terrible fever and finally died of it. I didn't know where else to find another cook. When Harry Paxton wrote he'd take the job, I accepted."

"Somebody else knew. Somebody else seems to know a lot," Fargo said.

Solita gave him a tolerant little smile. "Just opportunists looking for a chance at some money. That's all it is. Mark my words. Talk got out you were coming to me and they all decided they'd be better off if you didn't make it." Fargo said nothing in reply. Once again, the explanation fit too neatly, with too many coincidences for his stomach. Solita pushed to her feet with another graceful, lithe motion. He rose with her. "I appreciate your concern about my welfare, Fargo. I really do."

"I appreciate saving my own neck," he said and she tossed him a smile that held neither tolerance nor condescension as she hurried away. He took down his gear, shed his clothes, and slid into his bedroll. He was still awake when a sound came to his ears and he sat up, the Colt instantly in his hand. A figure came out of the darkness, wearing pajamas. With her short hair she could have been mistaken for a little boy. But the high breasts that pushed out the pajama top destroyed that possibility.

"Took me a while to find you," Clea murmured. "Just came to say good night and welcome, again." She let her eyes linger on the muscled beauty of his torso, then bent over to brush her lips against his, a promise more than an invitation, and then she was gone, hurrying away with a tomboy bounce to her step and a jiggle to her rear that not even her loose pajamas could hide. He lay back and thought about Clea and her uncle Harry. The attack on them had been no mistake. He was certain of that, now. But that didn't mean they knew anything more. They had seen a chance for a job and grabbed at it, only to find it had gotten them into trouble they hadn't bargained for.

Maybe it was over, now, Fargo pondered, but when he went to sleep he couldn't find any reassurance in that thought.

7

When morning came, Fargo was surveying the wagons as Solita joined him. Her raven hair swept against a pale pink shirt, an electric contrast of shimmering beauty. Under the morning sun, the golden glow was lighting her skin again with a new strength, and her long, slender figure seemed to glide beside him. Somehow, she managed to combine a prudish distance and a beckoning sensuality. She was, he decided, an unsettling mirror of contradictions. But she had chosen her wagons well—no unwieldy hard-to-handle Conestogas, he noted. Most of what she'd picked were Texas cotton bed rigs, deep-bodied and strong, with all their parts soaked in hot linseed oil before they were painted to withstand the dry, hot climate. A few had top bows for canvas covers that could be raised or lowered. Even Harry Paxton's wagon was a solid Owensboro farm rig, converted to a chuck wagon.

Matt Benton stopped by and again Fargo had the impression of a good but somewhat stolid man, made for taking orders. Solita obliged him by laying out directions in regal terms Matt Benton wouldn't dream of questioning. "You'll take the wagons straight north," Solita said. "A ten-minute break every hour, a half hour stop for lunch. Water will be rationed until we find a good supply. You can take an hour for minor breakdowns. Don't provoke trouble with Indians. Stay together. The guards ride at the rear of the last wagon." Matt Benton nodded respectfully and strode away, and Fargo soon felt Solita's eyes boring into him. "Want to share that smile with me?" she said, words more of a command than a question.

"Directions," he said. "They ought to be a guide, not a blueprint."

"You saying they were too detailed?" she pressed.

"Not for me but for him," Fargo said.

"What's that mean?" She frowned.

"You trust a man to be in charge, you trust him to make his own decisions, at the time, on the spot."

"Is that what you'd do?" she asked.

"Bull's-eye." He smiled.

She thought for a moment. "I'll let them stand. I like my decisions followed," she said.

"I'm sure, but that's not your real reason," Fargo said and she shot a hard glance at him. "You don't have confidence in Matt Benton to make the right decisions, that's what you're really saying. So you set down all the rules, make all the decisions."

Her dark eyes grew darker as they narrowed at him. "You think you can read me that easily?" she pushed at him.

"Hell no, just about some things." He grinned as

Benton began to move the wagons. Solita swung onto her horse, and Fargo saw she led a packhorse behind her with two large canvas sacks slung over its back, along with a leather pouch from which notepads protruded.

"We'll be riding on our own. They'll catch up with us later," she said and he swung in beside her as she set out on a path that took them out of sight of the wagons. "We'll make better time this way," she said.

"You seem to know where you're going," Fargo said.

"At the moment. I've some maps, most of them very primitive. We'll make one stop on the way to our main stop in this region."

"What's the main stop?" Fargo queried.

"The Seven Cities of Cibola," she said.

Fargo frowned at her. "They don't exist," he said.

"No, but Coronado thought they did. He wasn't the only one who did, either. A priest who'd sailed here with the Spanish force, a Father Marcos, claimed he had seen the golden cities from a distance. That was enough for Coronado," Solita said.

"You saying this Father Marcos lied?"

"Not exactly, more like he made a real mistake. It seems that when the sun hit just right, it reflected off of all the pieces of quartz in the walls of the adobe villages. From a distance, they looked as if they were made of gold, especially to those who wanted to see gold wherever they looked. When Coronado reached the place, all he found was the adobe villages. He'd gone there to find gold but he was also chasing the

Aztec warriors and they, too, had stopped there. So that's going to be one of our main stops. However, there was another place they stopped first. I want to go there, too, and be there before the wagons arrive so you can have a good look around," Solita explained.

Fargo allowed a rueful sigh. "And you expect I'm just going to look around and pick up a three-hundred-year old trail?"

"I've things to help. I'll show you when we get there. Let's get going," she said and put her horse into a canter, the packhorse following with a choppy gait. Anticipation and excitement had taken charge of her, he saw, her expedition finally started. He hung back, waiting until the pale pink shirt began to sprout darker spots as perspiration soaked into it. When her horse began to lather, he moved alongside her, leaned over, and took the horse's cheekstrap and pulled it to a halt. "What are you doing?" she asked sharply.

"You ride much farther like this in this country and you'll spend the rest of your time walking," he said. "Look at yourself. You're all sweated up already. So's your horse. You can't ride this far in this country at a canter."

Her frown faded and she glanced down at herself. "I guess I let excitement run away with judgment," she murmured.

"Excitement can do that," he said nonchalantly and she saw his eyes drop down to where the pale pink shirt had grown wet clinging to the line of her breasts, giving her taut nipples a new boldness.

"A gentleman wouldn't stare," she huffed.

"That wouldn't be a gentleman," he said.

"What would it be?"

"A damned fool." Fargo laughed and moved the Ovaro forward as Solita glared at him. When she caught up to him she had tucked a handkerchief into the front of her shirt.

"It'll absorb perspiration." She sniffed.

"And ruin a lovely view," he remarked.

"Now that you've brought it up I'm feeling very uncomfortable and sticky. Could you find one of those *tinajas*? I'd like to bathe and change before going on," Solita said.

"No," he said and drew another surprised glare. "In this country, *tinajas* are kept strictly for drinking. Drinking water is hard to come by out here. It's a kind of unwritten rule folks abide by."

"I see. Well, I shouldn't want to do the improper thing."

"Follow me," he said and turned the pinto north across the scorching, arid terrain, where striped-tailed scorpions and sand lizards were their only companions. When he saw the Maricopa Mountains rise up to his right, he turned west and finally heard Solita's little gasp of surprise and delight. "The Hassayampa River," Fargo stated, nodding at the slow-moving body of water lined with shadbush and peachleaf willow.

Solita dismounted at once, and took a towel and a pouch from her saddlebag and started toward the river, halting abruptly to stare at him. "You're not going to stand there and watch, are you?"

"Seems like a good idea," he said.

"Don't you have any respect, any manners at all?" she snapped.

"Respect is never to turn your back on beauty," he replied, "whether it's a sunset, a trumpet honeysuckle vine, a flock of indigo buntings, a fine palomino stallion—or a beautiful woman naked as a wood nymph. Beauty comes at unexpected times and unexpected places. It's a gift to enjoy, not to turn from."

"How high-minded," she said sarcastically. "Make an exception this time."

"That's asking a lot," Fargo murmured.

"Dammit, do you ever do the proper thing?" Solita spat.

"Do you ever say please?" he returned.

He watched her handsome face mirror the emotions that collided inside her; refusal, imperiousness, anger, frustration. But she called on her inner discipline and though her face remained reproachful, her voice grew soft. "Please," she said quietly.

"That wasn't so hard, was it?" He grinned, turning and walking away from her and the river shore. He heard her hurry on as he strolled out onto the land, his back to her though he could hear her splashing in the water. His eyes swept the dry Arizona territory, its very name an echo of Solita's Spanish conquistadores, being a Spanish rendering of the Pima Indians' name for the land, "the place of little springs." Little and few and far between, he grunted. Those Spanish invaders had to have learned the hard way that this was no land for cumbersome armies and heavy armor.

And now, hundreds of years later, the Apache showed how to use the land to fight and conquer and survive. Fargo's eyes narrowed at the thought, and swept the terrain. The Apache were never that far from anywhere in Arizona, always a threat seemingly appearing out of nowhere, bringing death with swift, silent efficiency.

But he glimpsed no signs of fleeting horsemen, though he had noticed more than enough unshod pony tracks to know that the Apache were here. That fact alone made Fargo uneasy. His eyes scanned the distant hills again, and he turned as he heard Solita coming toward him. She was still combing her jet black hair, which now hung long and loose. It gave her a very different look, he noted, another kind of beauty—a wildness added to her cool, patrician beauty. She had changed into a yellow shirt and when she reached him she set down her leather pouch and pulled her glistening raven hair back, tying it with a clip. "I like it loose. It changes you," he said.

"From what?" she asked.

"From cold to warm, from sensible to sensuous," he said.

"You think the way a woman wears her hair changes her?" she asked, amused.

"More than she wants to realize." He started to smile back.

"We've time to make up," she said, dismissing the topic and Fargo kept his smile to himself.

"Not at the expense of the horses," he said and she swung in beside him as he crossed east to the foothills of the Maricopa Mountains. There, he explored a passage through the low hills that cut time and distance, and brought them to the flat terrain where the wagons would soon be nearing.

"We need to look for a sandstone needle," Solita said.

"They usually grow out of pedestal rocks," Fargo said and his eyes scanned the line of rock formations at the bottom of the hills they had just left. When he spotted the tall, thin spire of sandstone, Solita grew excited at once.

"This is the place, on the other side of the needle," she said and he led the way past the spire along the broad, flat terrain.

"Do we wait for the others?" he asked.

"No, you start looking now," Solita said as she dismounted. "This is the first stop they made, both Coronado and the Aztec warriors they were chasing. That trail is here someplace."

"Was here," Fargo corrected. "Three hundred years of rain, wind, high country floods, and erosion have taken care of hoofprints, wagon wheel tracks, and foot marks. There's no way I can pick up a trail, not me, not the best Apache trackers, not anybody. I've been trying to tell you that from the start."

"There are other ways, other clues. I've things with me," Solita said, refusing to be dismissed. She stepped to the packhorse and fished into one of the sacks, drawing out a thick bundle of paper reinforced by cardboard backing. She brought one package to him and he saw that it was written in a combination of letters and symbols, none of which he could comprehend. "This is one of the old accounts that tell about Coronado's trail. Most are in Spanish, tales from survivors who returned with him. This is one of the few that are in Aztec," Solita said.

"Can you read the Aztec as well as the Spanish?" he asked and she nodded.

"I'm impressed. I'd rather learn more about you than a trail that's past finding," he said.

"It's not past finding," Solita said sharply. "I know it isn't. Find it and I'll tell you more about me." He allowed a tolerant smile as she held up the old piece of parchmentlike paper. "I'll read you what it says. I can't interpret it but I'm betting you can." He nodded, and didn't tell her she had more confidence in his abilities than he did. "Whoever wrote this had a basic understanding of what he saw, and he set down his simple impressions. First, he wrote: 'The plant you cannot touch.'"

Fargo smiled after a moment. "I'd guess that'd be a cactus. There are all kinds of cactus around here."

"Two heads taller than a man," Solita read aloud and Fargo frowned. "A gray beard that stings," she went on and his frown deepened. "Beauty in the darkness," she said next. "Then he drew a circle."

"That's it?" Fargo asked and she nodded and stepped back as he began to walk across the land, his eye squinting as he took in all that lay before him. He made his way through the creosote bush that covered a lot of the area, mixed in with gray-green brittlebush. He spotted barrel cactus, ocotillo shrubs, buckhorn cholla, the distant giant saguaros, and he paused at each of the other varieties of cactus. Jackrabbits leaped past him as he made a wide circle, then repeated it as Solita watched in silence. He had almost completed his second circle when he halted in front of a tall, delicate green cactus. He was studying it, a furrow creasing his brow, when Solita came alongside him.

"You've found something," she said.

"Maybe," he answered, his lips pursed as he stared again at the tall, delicate green of the plant. After a moment more, he turned to Solita. "Senita," he said. "Your writer was describing a Senita. They're about two heads taller than a man. They're sometimes call graybeards because the top of each stem is covered with a tuft of small stinging spines that grow like whiskers on a man's chin. They only blossom at night."

"Beauty in the darkness," she breathed softly.

"Exactly," he said.

"What's the circle mean?" she asked.

"That had me wondering, too, but look around you. This whole area is bounded by a wide circle of Senita cactus," he said.

Her eyes widened. "Yes, yes, it is," she said, turning as the wagons came into sight. She waved at them as they rolled up. As they pulled to a halt, Fargo stood back and she took command at once. First, she had the wagons draw back beyond the circle of the Senitas. "Diggers, start right at the center," she ordered. "Carefully, of course." He watched as she closely supervised the diggers beginning their work, staying close, paying careful attention to each hole as it was opened. They used small spades at first, switching to shovels and pickaxes.

Fargo strolled over to where Clea rested beside the chuck wagon, watching the diggers with almost as much attention as did Solita. "You're really caught up in this project," he commented.

"Mostly just curious," Clea said and linked her arm in his, bringing her tight figure firmly against him. "You find this spot for her?" she asked.

"She had some clues. I turned them into something more," he said.

"I thought about you all day. I thought we'd be riding together. I didn't know she was going to monopolize you," Clea said.

"She's paying and she's got plenty to be nervous about. If I can't produce, her whole project goes down the drain," Fargo replied.

"But you told her it was damn unlikely that even you could do what she wants," Clea said. "You changed your thinking on that?"

"Not really but I'm still going to try real hard. She deserves that," he said and Clea squeezed his arm.

"You're special, Fargo. She's lucky you're here," she said.

"Fargo, over here, please," he heard Solita call, her tone perfunctory. Clea disengaged herself from him with a tiny, smug smile as Fargo walked through the diggers and the careful excavations to where Solita waited. She handed him a notepad and pencil. "I must make a list of everything I find here now—plants, flowers, trees, animals, birds, everything. You could help a lot by setting down everything you see," she said. "If you can spare the time," she added tartly.

"Little testy, aren't we?" Fargo said mildly.

"Not at all. I just need your expert knowledge," she stated.

"Quick answers aren't always right answers." He laughed but she ignored his remark and returned to supervise the digging. As he began to make the list she wanted, he came to realize that it was very probable that the same plants, the same trees, flowers, animals, and birds were here three hundred years ago. As he watched a short-horned lizard make its way along the edge of the circle, he knew that its ancestors had traveled this way long ago, and that it had not changed one wrinkled, horny spine or leathered scale in hundreds of years. Certainly the land remained the same, and most of its creatures maintained their unique identity. Only humans changed in habit and character every generation.

By the time night began to descend, Fargo had completed his list, including a turkey vulture he had seen soaring in wide circles. When he brought Solita the list he saw the diggers beginning to fill in their holes. "Nothing worthwhile, I take it," he said.

"Coronado had stopped here. We found parts of helmets, a broken battle-ax, and half a dozen pieces of pottery of definite European design and material. They're being wrapped and put into one of the wagons now. Tomorrow, we go on to the Seven Cities," she said.

"What about the Aztecs he was chasing?" Fargo questioned.

"No sign of them. If they stopped here, they left nothing behind," she said. She started to turn away but Fargo stopped her.

"You've a short memory," he said as she frowned at him. "I made your piece of paper into a trail. You were going to tell me about yourself. That was the deal."

"Later, at supper. I'll come find you," she said and hurried away, her tall, lean figure swaying gently in the last rays of the day. A cooking fire was made and Fargo found a spot beyond the wagons, and watched Clea as she worked at the chuck wagon beside Harry Paxton. She stopped cleaning out a Dutch oven, and gazed at him with her hands on her hips, a half-amused, half-speculative glint in her light brown eyes.

"You're more tolerant than I'd have expected," she said.

"Meaning what?" he returned.

"You could've told Solita you were hired to find a trail, not catalog data for her," Clea said.

"That bother you?" He smiled.

"I don't like her attitude, the way she orders people around," Clea said.

"It's her way," Fargo said.

"You're sweet on her," Clea tossed at him.

"What the hell brings you to say a damned foolish thing like that?" he shot back.

"You make excuses for her. A man who makes excuses for a woman is sweet on her," Clea said.

"You really jump to conclusions, girl," he admonished.

"I just know what I see."

"You talk a lot of bullshit, honey," he said and laughed as he walked on. He finished his meal and strolled through the wagons, halting where Matt Benton lounged with the guards.

"How do, Fargo. The boss told me you pinpointed this place. That's damn good trail work," Benton said.

"I got lucky," Fargo said.

"It's never luck, from what I hear about you," Benton said and Fargo allowed a modest shrug as his eyes roamed over the guards. He looked for hard-eyed men who'd not do well taking Solita's orders, or hot-blooded youngsters who'd be anxious to show off—both the kind who could spell trouble. But he didn't see any. Nor did he see any with the fiery eyes of a sharpshooter or a hard case. They all seemed like solid types who'd do their job with everyday efficiency.

"Solita never exactly told me why she needed guards," Fargo said to Matt Benton as he quickly counted twenty figures.

"To protect the objects she expects she'll be finding," Benton replied. "Urns, vases, all kinds of pottery used by the Spanish and the Aztecs, weapons, armor, clothing. They'll be very valuable to collectors, she told me, and she wants to make sure they're not stolen. They'll be wrapped and carried in the wagons and these men will be guarding them, as well as the camp, against any *banditos*. Word has a way of getting out. She wants her things under guard."

"Smart," Fargo said, waving to the others as he strolled away. He found a spot beyond where the wagons were gathered, took out his bedroll, and had shed everything but his trousers when Solita appeared, a dark green, one-piece garment clinging to her supple form.

"You wanted to talk," she said, her tone flat, almost hostile, but he saw her eyes roam over his muscled torso.

"We made a deal," he reminded her, gesturing to the bedroll as he folded himself atop it. She dropped down beside him on her knees, the smooth silk of her garment flowing over her perky breasts.

"Yes." She nodded coolly. "That's why I'm here."

"You were going to tell me about Solita Chiltec," Fargo said. "How'd you come to know all about this piece of history?"

"A cousin got me interested," she said.

"Damn few people know about the Aztec," he said.

"I studied it," she responded.

"Where?" Fargo pressed.

"All over. From different people, all different places. Old people who know the old stories," Solita said.

"What's the name of the university that gave you the grant?" Fargo queried.

"I can't tell you that. They don't want to be embarrassed if I don't come up with anything. They don't want anything known about their part until I'm finished."

"What'd you do before getting into all this?" he questioned.

"Grew up," she said and pushed to her feet. He rose with her. "Enough questions. The interview's over," Solita said firmly as Fargo stood before her and watched her eyes move across his broad chest. Her hands came up, moved lightly across his pectoral muscles, then down to the tightness of his stomach, rising again to his biceps. "You would have been chosen," she said.

"Chosen?" he echoed.

"When the Aztecs fled Coronado's army, the high priests chose their strongest, handsomest, and most perfect warriors to carry the sacred objects. You would have been chosen as one of them," Solita said. "Maybe it's fitting that you are here, following their trail. The world moves in mysterious ways."

She turned and walked away in her smooth, gliding lilt, the garment undulating around her long legs as he watched until she vanished into the night. Fargo returned to his bedroll and stretched out, but his thoughts stayed on Solita's visit. She had answered his questions but had really told him nothing. Her answers had been cryptic, explaining little and revealing less. She'd made vague references to a cousin and old people with rumors. Then there was the university whose name couldn't be revealed for reasons that were conveniently ambiguous. Then there was an obscure period in which she "grew up." Everything couched in meaningless terms. Perhaps he was most bothered by her thinking he'd be so easily satisfied with her empty answers. His next question followed at once: Why did she have a need to be evasive? What was she hiding? And why?

He let the questions dance in his mind, finally pushing them aside, going to sleep determined to pursue a trail of his own tomorrow.

8

The morning sun woke him, and Fargo had just finished saddling the Ovaro when Clea appeared with a cup of coffee and a biscuit, handing both to him. He surveyed her as she stood before him, her short hair still wet from being washed, wearing a blue-gray shirt over blue-gray jeans, her hips slightly thrust forward. She could swagger standing still, Fargo noted silently, her snub-nosed face holding the edge of contrition. "Kind of a peace offering," she said.

"You taking back the idiot things you said?" he asked as he took a sip of the coffee.

"No," she huffed.

"That figures. You'd be too stubborn for that," he said.

"I just don't want you mad at me," she said.

"I'm not," he said and squeezed her shoulder, and continued finishing the biscuit and coffee. She suddenly reached up and kissed him, a quick, light brush of her lips, and then she spun and hurried away, her hips swaying, her high breasts bouncing. He finished breakfast and returned to the Ovaro to see Solita ride up, leading the packhorse behind her. She had the pale pink shirt back on and he smiled as he noticed that her jet black hair was not pulled back as severely as usual.

"Matt has been given directions. Let's go," she said abruptly. He swung beside her as she rode north, keeping the horses at a modest pace. She rode in silence for almost half an hour before she spoke, tossing words at him as she continued to stare straight ahead. "Do you want to tell your little admirer that nobody gets special treatment on this job, or should I?" she said.

Fargo let thoughts collect inside him for a moment, setting aside his first reaction to be biting. "Your show, your call," he simply said. He expected an answer but she fell back into silence until they reached the crumbling structures of the Pueblo dwellings as the sun passed the noon sky.

"The Seven Cities," Solita said.

"Must have been a helluva shock to Coronado," Fargo said. "Rock and dry scrabble ground." His gaze traveled over the stone structures and he did see a few places where imbedded pieces of quartz glinted faintly in the sun.

"By then, the Indian people had learned that the fastest way to get rid of the Spanish was to tell them where there was more gold. That's what they did with Coronado, sending him on with stories of gold further on," Solita said.

"What about the Aztecs he was chasing?" Fargo queried.

"He continued to try to do both. But the Aztecs stopped here before Coronado reached this place," Solita said, dismounting as a dozen figures appeared from the stone dwellings and started to advance toward them. They were mostly men, but Fargo saw some woman and a few near-naked children.

"Zuni," he said.

"Ashiwi," Solita said and drew a quick glance from him. "That's their tribal name, the name they had long before they were called Zuni." Fargo saw that the men and most of the women carried small objects in the stylized shape of animals and birds, bears, horses, wolves, badgers, doves, owls. They were all made of onyx, banded calcite, gypsum, carved antlers, graphite, and agate.

"Zuni fetishes. They'll try to use them to barter with us," he said and started to explain that the Zuni believed the fetishes were good luck charms with all kinds of power. She cut him off.

"*Wémawe*," she said.

"What's that?" he frowned.

"The Indian word for all fetishes. The Zunis are part of the Pueblo people and the Pueblo go directly back to the Inca, the Maya, and the Aztec. So do their fetishes. They call one of their main fetishes, usually carved from an antler, the fetish of the Feathered Serpent. In the time of the Inca, the Maya, and the Aztec, all of the Mexican peninsula was called the Land of the Feathered Serpent. Everything the Zuni do today relates back to those times. Today is yesterday in more ways than we know." Fargo's glance cut to the Zuni, who were still coming toward them. Solita walked over to the packhorse and took an object from one of the sacks. When she showed it to him, he saw it was remarkably similar to the carvings the Zunis held but it was a mountain lion made of yellow limestone. "*Wémahai*," she said, not bothering to explain further, and just started to walk toward the Zunis.

"Hold on," Fargo said in alarm. "They're not Comanche or Cheyenne but they can be real unfriendly." She didn't stop, and raised her hand and showed them the yellow limestone mountain lion figurine in her palm. The Zuni stared at the fetish for a moment, then backed away, almost running into the stone dwellings behind him. "What was all that?" Fargo asked.

"They recognized the *wémahai*, the strongest of all fetishes—the mountain lion, the God of the hunt fetish," she said.

Fargo's eyes narrowed at her. "You a collector, or a believer?" he asked.

"Both," she said with defiance in her black eyes. "There are things that go beyond what we understand. There are powers we do not recognize."

"Because they don't fit with our logic?" he said.

"Because we don't dare," she said, the defiance remaining in her eyes. He didn't reply, aware that her answer held more than he was ready to explore.

"Are all fetishes carved from some sort of stone or mineral?" he queried. "Seeing as how you seem to be an expert."

"Most, but not all. The *mili*, that's the fetish for

what the Zunis called the breath of life, a very important fetish, is a perfect ear of corn, filled with the seeds of sacred plants and wrapped in buckskin, then set in a basket and covered with the feathers of eagles, hawks, doves, and owls." She stepped to the packhorse and dropped the fetish into the sack. "They won't be bothering us. But we still have to find where the Aztecs stopped here. I want the exact spot, and I want to know what they left, if anything. And, of course, as with the last place, we need to write down all the plants, flowers, and animals that are in this place today. That'll apply to every dig we do."

Fargo's eyes traveled up and down the crumbling stone dwellings. "Unless you've some more clues, I don't see any way to pick up a trail here."

"I do have some things," Solita said, and dug into the sack and brought out another of the Aztec parchments. "Four clues, if you can find what they mean. I'll read them exactly as they were put down:

"When the land stops burning.
Like man but not like man.
Marks of darkness.
A place no more."

"Why is everything so damned cryptic?" Fargo asked.

"They wanted to leave a record, but not for Coronado or anyone else following him," Solita explained.

Fargo grunted unhappily as he repeated the phrases in his mind and began to walk the stretch of cliff dwellings, Solita tagging along. Most were partly crumbled, and he led the way into each of the stone houses. The rooms were mostly small and square, some with T-shaped windows. But as they explored further, a large, circular room appeared. "A *kiva*, a ceremonial room," he said, and noted the sandstone walls where mud had been used as the mortising material.

"Why have they deteriorated so? Just from erosion? They're not thousands of years old," Solita asked.

"Climate and natural conditions speed erosion," he said, and knelt down on one knee to show her long paths where the ground was marked by unusual smoothness. "Water ran through here once. Not a lot, but more than enough for those who lived here to make repairs and build new dwellings. Then something happened. The water stopped, forever. Without water, there was only the sun-baked dryness. With only the wind and the sun, the stones began to crumble, and there was no water with which to make more mud cement. I'd guess the people who lived here left to find another place." Fargo rose, and showed her a gnarled, petrified stump. "There were trees here once, too. Again, not many, but enough. Paloverde and juniper, I'd guess," he said. She nodded, her face tight, as the wagons rolled into view. "Maybe we'd do best to just go on," he suggested.

"No," she said sharply. "They stopped here. I have to find the spot. I can't pass up one place. That's what I agreed to. You work on what these clues mean," she insisted, holding up the piece of parchment.

"It'll take time, if I can figure it out at all," Fargo said.

"Whatever time you need," she said and strode away to meet the wagons. She was directing them where to pull in far enough away from the stone dwellings as Fargo walked on to the far end of the structures. Slowly, he began to walk from one to another once again, going into each one, surveying everything he saw inside. When he went outside, his trailsman's eyes swept the loose, dry soil as the four cryptic clues revolved inside him. He studied every small rise and fall in the soil, every mark that showed itself, and the footprints of every creature that still walked the land. This was a land and a place where little changed except man and his restless ways. The land and its creatures had little need to change their ways.

He had twice gone the length of the dwellings and twice examined the land and every mark upon it when night fell. He stopped to get a tin plate and some food at the chuck wagon. Clea moved forward to serve him and he saw a hint of defiance in the way she piled his plate high. "Should I make a guess?" he slid at her.

"She stopped by," Clea said tightly.

"Had a word about special treatment?" Fargo asked.

"She can go to hell," Clea hissed and put another spoonful of potatoes on his plate. "I do what I want, when I want. I hope she's watching."

"Simmer down, girl," Fargo heard Harry Paxton say.

"Thanks," Fargo said and stepped aside as Matt Benton stepped into line with his plate. Benton then came to sit with Fargo as he ate.

"Hope you come up with something soon, Fargo," Benton said. "The men are getting bored, especially the guards. Solita doesn't seem to know what kind of trouble that can bring."

"She knows. She just won't tolerate the thought. She expects the men to do their jobs, bored or not," Fargo said. "Tell them to be patient."

"What's that mean?"

"Nothing I can pin down, except that this trail is taking us into some real unfriendly country," Fargo said.

"If you're talking about Indians, most of the men have had some experience Indian fighting. I already asked about that," Benton said.

"What Indians?" Fargo queried.

"Paiute, Kickapoo, Choctaw, Potawatami, Iowa. I myself have tangled with Osage and Shawnee," Benton said. "I guess none of us have ever run into the big Plains tribes."

"Ever fight the Comanche?"

"No," the man said.

"They're the worst, or the best, depending on how you want to look at it. An old scout I once knew said you always want to see a Comanche before he sees you, and when you do you're still sorry you saw him. I've a feeling we'll be seeing them," Fargo said, and left Matt Benton to finish his meal alone. Returning to the chuck wagon, Fargo tossed his plate into the wreck pan as Clea came around the rear of the wagon. Hardly pausing, she passed close beside him, let her arm encircle his waist and then was gone, hurrying away. Fargo walked on surveying the cliff houses once more before finally taking to his bedroll. As he undressed and lay down, Fargo watched the moonlight bathe the land in its pale silver, eerily lighting the crumbling stones and the land.

He had found nothing to make sense out of any of the veiled Aztec writings but he had become convinced that if he could find the answer to one, the rest would fall into place. Yet he hadn't the answer to any, and he cursed silently and kept staring out at the land awash in moonlight as if it would suddenly fling an answer out at him. Finally, Fargo closed his eyes and fell asleep.

The moon had passed the midnight mark, still bathing the land in its pale yet softly clear light when Fargo suddenly snapped awake. He sat bolt upright, feeling the thoughts exploding inside him as he stared out at the land and the stone dwellings. "Damn!" he breathed as he leaped to his feet. "Damn, that's it!" Excitement swirled through him as he pulled on clothes and hurried toward the dwellings, halting before he reached them, his eyes peering at the ground. He stayed frozen in place, watching, observing, listening, until he spun and strode toward the silent wagons. He searched quickly, and finally spied Solita wrapped in a blanket outside the line of wagons, her two horses nearby.

She woke as he halted beside her, blinking sleep from her eyes as she sat up, her raven hair flowing long and loose around her face and neck. She wore a robe of light, off white cotton, he saw, and she just stared at him. "What is it?" she asked, surprise and an edge of alarm in her voice.

"Get up," he said. "I've got it." Her eyes widened instantly and she started to push to her feet. The top of her robe dipped and he glimpsed the line of one softly curving breast as she rose. She started to pull the robe off and caught herself and stopped. Her eyes looked into Fargo's, quietly commanding him, and he turned his back on her. She pulled on her clothes quickly, donning a tan shirt and riding britches, and then came beside him. "Look out there," he said. "What don't you see? What's missing?"

She frowned out at the scene for a moment. "The sun. It's night. I'm not being scorched," she said, then halted with a soft gasp and turned to him as her lips fell open and her eyes grew wide. "When the land stops burning," she breathed, awe in her voice.

"Bull's-eye," he said. "It was there, right in front of me, but I couldn't put it together. It hit me when I was asleep. It's the key to everything else."

"How?" she asked as he took her by the elbow and pulled her across the thin, loose layer of sandy soil over the rock beneath. Pulling the notepad she'd given him from his pocket, he started to draw three sets of paw prints, then handed the pad to her when he finished.

"These critters are all over this region. I've marked each print. Look at the tracks they make. Take your time. Look carefully." His eyes narrowed, he followed her gaze as she studied each of the tracks. "The first one's an ordinary brown rat. They're everywhere, in the woodland and the desert," he said. "The second's a desert rat."

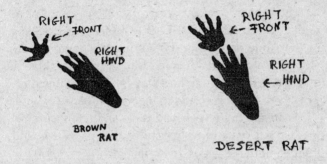

"The third is a kangaroo rat," Fargo said.

He waited as she studied the three sets of tracks, finally interrupting her intense thoughts. "What's different about the third set?" he asked. She took a moment more, then answered.

"There are no tracks for the front paws," she said.

"Bull's-eye, again. The kangaroo rat hops on its rear feet. It moves on two feet, not four," Fargo said.

Solita's eyes grew wide again as she looked at him, her words soft and again full of awe. "Like man but not like man," she breathed.

"Exactly," Fargo nodded.

"What about the next one, 'marks of darkness'?"

"The kangaroo rat is nocturnal. It leaves its tracks at night," Fargo said and led her to a place near the last of the stone dwellings. Twenty or so kangaroo rats stopped catching red-banded leafhoppers, cinchbugs, and crane flies, scurrying away in fright as they approached. Fargo gestured to the wide expanse of land. "This area is full of petrified roots and a few stumps. It was once a stand of trees, probably paloverde and juniper, until the water dried up."

"A place no more," Solita said and Fargo nodded.

"You can start digging here come morning," he said and walked back with her, halting beside her blanket.

"I was sure you'd find the key," she said with a hint of smugness.

"I sure wasn't," he admitted.

"Because you believe in training, experience, knowledge. I believe in a lot more," she said. "We've a few hours till morning. I'm going back to sleep."

He left as she turned away, walking to his bedroll to take advantage of the few hours to sleep. When he woke, his conclusions hadn't changed. Luck played as large a part in the events of the night before as did experience. He wondered how long that luck would last, and wanted to dismiss Solita's blithe confidence as unrealistic optimism. But something about her eagerness refused to allow that as he strolled to where the diggers were already at work, unearthing the entire area. It was noon before they made their first find—the bleached bones of four skeletons in different locations within what appeared to be a series of connecting tunnels. Solita dropped down into the hole and examined the vestiges of clothing still clinging to the bones, along with three jeweled wrist ornaments. "Aztecs," she said. "Keep searching."

She stayed down with the diggers as Fargo watched from above, noting that almost two dozen Zunis watched from a distance. By the close of the day, the site had been thoroughly excavated. They had found a clay urn, three drinking utensils, and the point of a Spanish lance. The finds were carefully wrapped, then placed into one of the wagons as the excavations were filled in. "You didn't find much," Fargo said to Solita.

"Enough to know they were here and Coronado didn't get anything," Solita said. "The Aztecs we found had obviously stayed on as decoys while the others got away. Let's get on cataloging whatever we found here."

She walked away from him, contained and composed. She had covered her disappointment in her patrician face well. But Fargo had still seen it in her eyes, and he wondered what it meant. She was trying to reconstruct a trail, reconcile and compare the past with the present. Objective curiosity would have been normal, not disappointment. The thought played on Fargo's mind as he began to fill his list with insects, rodents, plants, and birds. When night came, he fell into a restless, unsatisfied sleep. Come morning, Solita sought him out as he watched Matt Benton prepare the wagons to move out. "We'll be going east, into New Mexico. My primitive map shows that they went to what's now called Albuquerque," she said. "That's where we'll go. I expect you'll take us there."

He nodded. He was growing accustomed to how she could make a statement sound like a flat-out command. With a wave to Benton, Fargo started off across the flatland, the line of wagons and riders following closely. They fell behind when Fargo crossed into New Mexico, as they had to steer around the long clusters of giant saguaros and cholla bushes that dotted the terrain. A trickle of a stream afforded them a place to water the horses, and as Clea passed them driving the chuck wagon, she flashed Fargo a bright smile she knew Solita would see. When Fargo moved the caravan forward again, the sun was well into the midafternoon sky, and the land began to rise. It quickly grew thick with juniper, paloverde, stunted hackberry, and twisted oaks. They had reached the Mangas Mountains and Fargo waved the wagons forward up into the mountain passes.

"It's the most direct route to Albuquerque," he told Solita. "It also has one of the best passages across the Continental Divide."

"Yes, the Aztec warriors took it. Coronado followed, of course," Solita said.

"If the wagons can make it, we will, too," Fargo said.

"And if they can't?" she questioned.

"We might have to take them apart, work a kind of portage," he said and she showed her displeasure at the prospect. Fargo continued to lead the wagons forward as he scanned the higher passages for those wide enough for their caravan. His options were quickly growing smaller, he noted. But he also scanned the passages that spread out below them, using the distant peak of Escondido Mountain as a beacon. Moving slowly ever higher, he glanced back and sought out the chuck wagon. It was perhaps the most solid of all the wagons, but also the most cumbersome. But Harry Paxton held the reins steady. Fargo turned away and sent the Ovaro forward, leaving the wagons to make their slow climb. Solita came up to ride beside him as he suddenly reined to a halt. Fargo dismounted and picked up a torn piece of buckskin gauntlet. "Comanche," he said, and immediately swept the high land with a long glance.

"I haven't seen anyone or anything," Solita said.

"With the Comanche, that doesn't mean anything," Fargo snapped and walked forward to where he spotted the pony prints. Six horses, he noted, kneeling down and running his fingers over the edges of the prints. They crumbled at his touch. "They're not fresh," he said gratefully. Swinging into the saddle, he moved forward, glancing back at the wagons moving slowly up the increasingly steep passage. They were beginning to near the great chasm of the Continental Divide, the Tulla Tosa Mountains at their rear, now. Fargo had been riding a few paces ahead of Solita when he heard the cry of a woman's voice from the passages below.

He moved to where he could peer down and saw a covered Texas seedbed wagon hanging half over the edge of the cliff. The horses were gone. Either they had broken free or gone over the cliff. Two men were desperately hanging on to the tailgate of the wagon with ropes. Two women in bonnets and long dresses were draped over the side of the wagon, plainly injured. Two more women in bonnets lay unmoving on the ground, and another woman waved frantically at him. "They're in real trouble. Send the others when they get here. I'm going down," Fargo said.

"No," Solita said sharply and swung from her horse.

"What?" Fargo frowned incredulously.

"I said no," she repeated firmly.

"You've got to be kidding," Fargo said.

"I'm not kidding. You're not going down there," she said, ice coating each word.

"They need help. Every second counts," Fargo said.

"No," Solita said again, her face a beautiful, yet frosty mask. "You keep going. You've no time to play Good Samaritan. Move on."

He stared at her, unable to believe his ears as fury erupted inside him. "Go to hell, honey," he bit out.

"You'll do as I say. You're working for me, Fargo, remember?"

"I quit," he flung at her.

She surprised him as her hand slapped his face hard. "No, you don't. I set the rules here."

"And I hit back," he snapped, swiping his palm

across her face just hard enough to redden her cheek and see her eyes widen in surprise. He spun, walked to the edge of the passage in two strides, and peered down again. The two men were still desperately hanging on to the ropes tied to the wagon, but it wouldn't be long before it went over the cliff. He wondered if there were others inside it, was about to start over the edge to scramble down the side when Solita's voice speared into him.

"Don't, Fargo. Dammit, I'll shoot."

He turned and saw the rimfire derringer pointed at him. She wouldn't miss at this range, he knew. He let his arms drop to his sides, gave a little shrug of resignation, and took a step toward her. "Guess you mean it," he said. "You win." He took another step closer, letting submission slide across his face. The barrel of the derringer dropped down for only a second, but the moment was all he needed. Few diamondbacks struck any faster, a low, flashing motion underneath the gun, tackling her legs. She went down, too surprised to squeeze the trigger, and he was quickly atop her, tearing the little gun from her hand. He sprang up as she pushed to her feet. "You're really a rotten little bitch, as evil as you're beautiful," he flung at her. Emptying the little pistol, he threw it at her feet, then whirled and ran back to the edge of the road.

He scrambled down the steep side, slowing his headlong plunge by grabbing on to the ends of mountain shrubs. When he landed on the narrow ledge near the wagon, the woman who had been waving turned toward him, and the two women who had been draped over the side of the wagon suddenly pulled themselves up. Both came up holding rifles, he saw with astonishment. The rifles barked and two bullets hurtled past him and he threw himself on the ground, rolling for a line of low, mountain shrub. As he reached the shrubs, he glimpsed the two men yanking their six-guns out as they let go of the wagon. Fargo cursed, and rolled deeper into the low line of shrubs as more bullets plowed into the ground only inches from him. Peering through the shrubs, he saw that two of the women had lost their bonnets, and he saw that they had short hair and three-day stubble on very masculine jaws.

They were all pouring lead into the shrubs now, and Fargo flattened himself on the ground. He cursed bitterly. It had been a trap and he had plunged into it and now he was pinned down. He needed a tree, a rock, any place to let him move and return fire. The shrubs were too low. They'd see him if he rose to fire. As he silently cursed, he realized they were starting to bracket their fire, working their way toward him from both ends of the line of bushes. They'd be certain to reach where he lay and he debated leaping up, shooting furiously, and making a run for it. He could get lucky but he didn't ever like depending on luck.

Another volley of shots reminded him that perhaps he had little choice left. He gathered himself and raised the Colt when a single, heavy-duty rifle shot exploded from not too far away. He heard a man's voice curse in pain, then the sound of a body falling heavily to the ground. Another of the deafening shots rang out, this one followed by a guttural cry and then the kind of silence that only means death. Fargo lifted his head and peered through the top of the bushes as still another shot exploded. He saw one of the men in a women's dress grab his shoulder, curse, and fall to one knee, then stagger to his feet and start to run. One of the other men in women's clothing rose and began to back away.

Fargo drew a quick bead on the disguised woman and fired, and the figure bucked and collapsed on the ground. Seizing the opportunity, Fargo threw himself backward out of the shrubs, seeing a low rock and diving behind it. Two more of the men in drag rose and started to run. The unseen rifleman fired twice and both running figures pitched forward and lay still. Silence swept over the scene and Fargo let a moment pass before he rose, stepping out from behind the rock, the Colt raised and ready to fire. He glimpsed a movement from behind a cluster of dwarf oaks, and then a small figure swaggered out, her peering, snub-nosed face searching him out.

"Surprise," she said.

"And a damn nice one," he answered and Clea was beside him in two quick strides, her arms quickly circling around him, her round softness pressed tightly against him. She carried a big, old Hawken plains rifle, which explained the heavy blast of gunfire. Her lips found his—no quick, light touch this time, but lingering with soft warmth and intensity until she pulled away.

"It's my turn to say thanks," he said.

"Guess this kind of makes us even," Clea murmured.

"Guess so," he agreed.

"We all heard the shooting. The others went up the high road, the way you'd gone. I climbed down to the low road," Clea said.

"I'm sure glad for that," Fargo said and Clea glanced down at the disguised figures sprawled life-lessly on the ground.

"Who are they and why are they dressed as women?" she asked.

"Don't know but it was no accident," he said.

"Meaning what?" she queried.

"Don't know exactly, but they were no passing *banditos*. This was planned, right down to the disguises," he said darkly. "One more thing that sticks in me."

"What do you mean?" she asked.

"It's one more thing that doesn't fit. Why have there been so many damn attempts at stopping some-body on a scholarly examination of a three-hundred-year-old trail?" he said.

"I wouldn't know about that," Clea said and he shot her a curious glance. Her answer had been too quick and too defensive. He tabled the surprise that nipped at him as Matt Benton's voice called out. Fargo saw him with two of the guards at the edge of the high pass above them.

"Grab hold of this," Benton called as he lowered a rope. Fargo strode to the steep side of the mountain and had them pull Clea up first, then pulled himself up on the rope as it was lowered again. "Sorry I didn't get here sooner," Benton said.

"It's over. That's all that counts," Fargo said. As

Clea sauntered back to the chuck wagon in a slow swagger, Fargo walked to where Solita waited a dozen yards behind the wagons. She regarded him from under her high, arched eyebrows with regal disapproval, but her black eyes held no smoldering fire.

"You were completely out of line," she said reprimandingly.

"And you're sure as hell not off the hook," he threw back.

"Why not?" She frowned.

"You didn't know they weren't what they seemed to be—people in desperate need of help," he said.

"I knew," she said quietly.

He frowned harder at her. "You knew? What the hell does that mean?"

"I didn't know the exact spot or the precise way they would try, but I knew," she said with unruffled assurance.

"Make some sense," he said angrily.

"This is a place of deceit and betrayal," she said.

"You really mean that," he said, peering at her.

"Absolutely. It is written that Coronado met with the Aztecs he was pursuing somewhere near here in these mountains, perhaps in this exact same place. He told them he wanted only peace. He told them that his men were exhausted and tired, that he was giving up the pursuit. To prove his words, he gave up his guns and armor. The Aztecs believed him, and accepted the gesture. But he had more guns hidden and he attacked and killed half the Aztec warriors. The

139

other half managed to get away and run. Betrayal and deceit. This is a place marked by the spirit of both."

"You really believe such power—a spirit—exists? That it can have a spell over a place or a time?" Fargo asked.

"I believe in powers we do not fully comprehend," she said. "Wasn't it just proven?"

"Coincidence," he said.

She returned a patronizing smile. "How much easier is it for you to live with that explanation," she said.

He studied her calm, patrician loveliness. "You're different from anyone I've ever known, I'll say that," he remarked. "Why didn't you tell me you felt this way before pulling your derringer?"

"Would you have listened? Would you have believed me?" she tossed back reproachfully. "No, you would have just said I was making up stories to stop you from playing Good Samaritan." He grimaced at the truth in her words, and started to turn away when he found her right behind him, her voice suddenly soft. "Am I still a rotten bitch?" she slid at him.

"I guess I'll be taking that back," he said.

"What am I then?" she pressed.

"A package of surprises. That's the best I can do," he said.

"I'll settle for that," she and he peered hard at her, trying to see behind that cool, composed facade. It was like fire with a wall of frost around it, he concluded, and brought his eyes to the surroundings. The sun still bathed the tall sides of the towering Continental Divide, with Allegros Mountain directly to the north. But the sun's position told him something more. "We'll never make it across the divide before nightfall, and we sure can't tackle the mountains on the other side by dark," he told Solita. "There's a wide stream halfway across. We should make camp there." She nodded as Fargo's glance cut to the tall, rugged mountains that formed the other side of the great Continental Divide as it zigzagged from north to south. Suddenly his eyes widened, narrowing instantly. A flash had come from halfway up the nearest mountainside, the briefest explosion of light. He focused on the spot and it flashed again, for a split second and then it was gone.

But Fargo knew its meaning and his jaw grew tight. The last of the sun's rays had glinted off something—a piece of metal, the blade of a knife, an amulet of quartz, perhaps the polished surface of a beartooth necklace, but something not of tree, bush, or flower. "Where are you going?" Solita asked as he turned the Ovaro.

"Exploring. Meet you when you make camp," he said and hurried off before she had time to question him further. He never believed in causing alarm until it was necessary. There was always the chance that the sun had flashed on a piece of mirror dropped by someone crossing the mountains, he told himself, but his face stayed tight as he sent the Ovaro up a path through a heavy growth of burr oak.

9

He was grateful for the thickening tree cover as the mountainside rose—sycamore, juniper, and gambel oak along with plenty of hardy mountain shrub. Circling to the side of the mountain where he had glimpsed the flashes of sun, he sent the Ovaro up narrow paths through the trees until he reached a midway spot on the mountain. He stopped climbing and began to move the horse horizontally across the slope. The tree cover began to thin out somewhat, the oak and sycamore giving way to good browsing shrubs, white ratany, baby bonnet, and false mesquite. Where rocky ridges began to protrude, he saw growths of orange-edged woolly lipferns, a fern able to grow where no others could.

He was carefully edging his way along the slope when suddenly, not more than a hundred feet away, the flash of sunlight blazed again. This time he was close enough to pinpoint the spot, beside a jutting piece of rock flanked on both sides by old, gnarled oaks. He lowered himself from the saddle and crept forward on foot, glancing at the land below. Though

the sun had left the valley, he could make out the wagons slowly rolling near the stream. A movement
caught the corner of his eye, and then he discerned the
figure step out from behind the rock. Not very tall, the
figure was clad only in frayed, buckskin trousers, the
rest of his lithe, muscled body naked. His shoulder-
length hair, black and unruly, framed the flat, taut,
high-cheekboned, reddish brown face of the typical
Comanche.

A cartridge belt lay diagonally across his chest and
as he stepped forward, a last ray of sun flashed
against one of the cartridges. Fargo let a grim smile
touch his lips. Even a Comanche could be careless. As
he watched, the Indian crouched and peered down at
the wagons below. Fargo glimpsed that the rifle in his
hand was an army carbine. Not bought at an army
supply depot. As the Comanche turned, Fargo saw
the hunting knife he kept in a waist sheath. Lifting his
eyes, Fargo quickly swept the mountain beyond
where the man crouched. No other figures met his
search—the Indian was a lone scout. The Comanche
favored sending lone scouts, young warriors trained
to go days without food or water, if need be.

This one could not be allowed to report the wagons
to his chief, Fargo knew as he crept forward again.
The Indian's rifle held the key to success or failure. He
was alone but a shot would echo through the mountains for miles. The alarm would be sent even if he
never brought it by word. Fargo eyed the carbine in
the man's hand seeing that the Indian was holding it
loosely. He had no reason not to as he peered down at

the wagons moving below his perch. Fargo's hand stole down to the double-edged, thin throwing knife in the calf holster around his leg, his fingers curling around the blade of the weapon. But he then released the knife and drew his hand back. He didn't have a clear shot, one that was certain to be instantly fatal. Anything less would give the Comanche time to fire his carbine.

Fargo's hand touched the butt of the Colt and just as quickly moved away. He could bring the Indian down with a single shot, but it would raise the alarm to other Comanches, whether it came from his gun or the Indian's carbine. He had to close in on the Comanche, and wrestle the weapon from him before he had a chance to fire. Cursing inwardly, Fargo crept forward again, inching his way step by step. The Indian turned from where he'd been peering down at the wagons below and began to move toward the rock. Fargo's eyes followed him and spotted the horse partly concealed behind the rock, a rugged, dun pony. The man moved with short steps. He'd be at the horse in moments. Fargo moved quickly, too quickly. His foot dislodged a pebble and it rolled with what seemed the sound of thunder.

The Comanche spun at once, frowning, his eyes sweeping the surroundings. Still behind an oak, Fargo froze in place. But he knew there was suddenly no time left, only split seconds in which to win or die. The Comanche took a step closer, every muscle in his lean, tight body tense, his instinct telling him that danger was imminent. Gathering every bit of power in his muscled legs, Fargo catapulted himself forward from behind of the tree, hurtling through the air like some unearthly combination of wild man and battering ram. He slammed into the Indian and the man's smaller, lighter figure sailed backward. He hit the ground hard, Fargo atop him, the breath knocked from him for an instant.

The Comanche managed to get a knee up, and tried to shove Fargo off of him but Fargo had one hand on the stock of the carbine. Twisting, he used the leverage of his long arms and tore the weapon from the man's hands. Pushing to his feet, he flung the gun into the air and heard it crash down the mountainside. He whirled to see the Comanche on his feet, drawing the hunting knife. The Indian came in on quick catlike steps, sending a swiping blow that Fargo easily avoided. The Indian lashed out again from the other direction and Fargo avoided the blow with the same ease. He frowned as the Indian tried another loping blow, feinting right, then left, seeming to prepare for another swiping attack. But a flash of suspicion flamed inside Fargo and he looked down at the man's feet just in time to see them change position. He was able to see the hunting knife plunge straight forward as the Comanche leaped right at him. Fargo twisted, drawing his stomach in, and the blow went past.

But the Comanche whirled, leaping forward again, the hunting knife thrust straight forward. Again, Fargo pulled away and the blade hurtled inches past his midsection. But this time, Fargo brought a pile driver blow down on the Indian's forearm as it flew past. The Comanche let out a grunt of pain as the blade clattered from his hand. Fargo's next blow was a massive roundhouse right that smashed into the Indian's back with tremendous force. It was a blow that would break the back of the average man, and it landed flush on the Indian's spine. He let out a scream of agony, pitched forward a half-dozen steps and went down hard on his face.

Fargo strode over to him and saw that the Comanche had managed to turn over on his back, his face still contorted in pain. The Indian kicked one leg up and out, his blow catching Fargo in the groin, and it was Fargo's turn to grunt in pain as he dropped to one knee. Taking a moment to shake away the pain that spread like wildfire throughout his lower torso, he saw the Comanche crawl, stumbling forward to retrieve the knife and rise to his feet in a pained crouch.

Cold fury in his black eyes, the Indian came at him again, and Fargo found himself in awe of the superb conditioning and inner tenacity that let the Comanche keep on after a blow that would have left most men unable to move. Hunting knife raised, the Comanche lashed out with short, flat blows. Fargo backed up, reached down, and yanked the thin, double-edged throwing knife from his calf holster. He could take no more risks, as his opponent was too dangerous, too consumed in hate. When Fargo drew the knife, the Comanche instantly saw it for what it was and didn't back away as the average man would have. With the training and instincts of a seasoned

146

warrior, he came forward, knowing that a throwing knife needs room to be thrown. Rushing in, striking out with furious, short thrusts of the hunting knife, the Indian crowded Fargo, who had to back away. But the Comanche kept crowding him, lashing out with his heavier, wider blade.

Fargo tried a short, straight jab at the man's naked midsection, but the Indian used his hunting knife to deftly parry the thrust and Fargo had to twist away from a return blow. The Comanche was almost atop him instantly, crowding him with one short, chopping swipe of his knife after another. Fargo kept backtracking, running out of room before he suddenly saw something. The Indian's body never straightened up. For all his quick slashes and thrusts, he never stood erect. Fargo's thoughts flew to the pile driver blow he had smashed into the man's spine. It hadn't done what it would have to most men, but Fargo suddenly realized it hadn't been entirely ineffective, either. The Indian was fighting with a badly injured spine. He could manage short steps, fight in close where he didn't have to straighten up, somehow fighting through torturous pain. But he couldn't run.

Fargo stopped backing away, and spun around and began to run full out. When he halted to whirl around again, the Comanche was a dozen feet from him, trying to follow, but his body was badly twisted as he moved forward, his pain-wracked, shuffling gait the best he could manage. Now, with the room he needed, Fargo used an underhand throw to send the thin blade hurtling through the air. The Comanche saw the blade coming at him but he could give only a cry of excruciating pain as he tried to turn aside. His movements far too slow, his face contorted as the throwing knife all but disappeared into his side. Slowly, he dropped to both knees, swaying there for a moment before pitching forward to lie facedown, still.

Fargo drew a deep breath and walked slowly to the motionless figure, retrieving the blade and wiping it clean on a bush before making his way to the Ovaro. This much was over. He had done what he needed to do—buy time. The others would come searching for their scout when he didn't return. But that wouldn't be for another day, perhaps two—enough to get the wagons out of the bottom of the divide. He rode back down the mountainside as night fell, and spied the cooking fire, finding the wagons spread out alongside the stream. Matt Benton and Solita were in line to be served at the chuck wagon when Fargo arrived. He saw Clea half hidden behind Harry, who was busy dishing out supper.

"Finished exploring?" Solita asked.

"For now," Fargo said, taking a tin plate to stand in line behind Benton.

"Find anything?" Solita questioned.

Fargo hesitated, and decided that the truth wouldn't risk setting off an alarm, for now. "There was a Comanche," he said and was surprised to see concern touch only Matt Benton's face.

"Should we set out night sentries?" Benton asked. "Just in case?"

"No, I took care of him. I figure we'll be out of here before they come looking for him," Fargo said.

"The Comanche won't be a problem," Solita said serenely.

"Glad you're so sure of that," Fargo said.

"I have the mountain lion fetish, remember? Though you're a skeptic, Fargo, I remind you what effect it had on the Zunis," she said.

Fargo's smile held a wry bitterness. "The Comanche aren't the Zuni. Different breed of cat," he said.

"You'll see," she said with smug confidence as Harry Paxton served her and Fargo walked away, reminding himself that Solita was a strange combination of mystic and pragmatist. He took the Ovaro past the wagons to a stubby sycamore tree near the stream and settled his gear down. Supper was nearly over when he returned to the chuck wagon and Clea hurried up to serve him.

"I've a pup tent I was going to pitch tonight off by itself, way past the last wagon. Then I heard you talking about Comanches," she said.

"You'll be safe enough tonight," he told her.

"I'd feel safer if you came visiting," she said softly, a tiny smile relaying its own message.

"Wouldn't want you not to feel safe," he said evenly as he strolled away. Later, he set out his bedroll and let the camp grow still before he rose and wandered down the edge of the stream past the last wagon. He finally spied the small pup tent set back of the stream beside a cluster of juniper. The faint glow of a candle flickered against the canvas from inside. He pulled the tent flap aside to see Clea seated atop a cot, her tomboy figure only partly covered by a short nightgown that let him see legs that were well muscled, nicely curved thighs, rounded knees, and shapely calves. She brushed her short hair back as he entered the tent, then reached out and drew him down to the cot beside her. Her lips found his at once, pressing hard against him.

"You don't believe in wasting time," he commented.

"Not when time is precious. Not when I've been hungering," she said.

"Is that what you've been doing?" Fargo asked.

"Ever since that first day," she said. "When you turned up here, I knew it was some kind of sign." Clea's fingers unbuttoned his shirt quickly and deftly, and when she finished, she pushed it from him and her palms moved across his smoothly muscled chest, pressing, lingering. The flats of her palms were warm against him as they slid slowly down his chest. He undid his gunbelt and trousers, casting both aside as her hands slid down further. Clea's touch was both firm and soft, controlled yet with a slight trembling that transmitted its own special kind of excitement. He felt his body responding and when her hands reached his groin, she gasped, drawing back only long enough to fling the short nightgown over her head.

He took in her breasts, smallish but very high and apple-round, each standing out perfectly, each light pink tip surrounded by a lighter pink circle. Narrow but very rounded hips followed a small waist where a tiny elliptical indentation offered its own provocativeness. Her slightly convex belly seemed designed for stroking and just below it, a surprising triangle seemed to contradict her tomboy litheness, a very dense, bushy, black assertion of female sensuousness. Her hands ran down his body again, finding him once more and she cried out as her fingers clasped tightly around his stiff rod, moving up and down his maleness until, with an almost impatient little sound, she lifted herself up, sliding up along his body and bringing her round, firm breasts to his face. His lips quickly found one light pink nipple tip and encircled it, pulling at it gently as Clea gasped out.

"Uuummmm . . . yes, oh, oooh, oh, God, yes, ummmm," she breathed as he took the small, firm mound deeper into his mouth, caressing it gently, reveling in the sweet taste of her. "Oh, Jeeez, Jeez," Clea moaned and her back arched as she pushed herself upward, deeper into his mouth. She was writhing when he pulled away and let his lips trace a path across her breasts, down along her abdomen, pausing at the little indentation of her cleavage, caressing it. "Yes, oh, go on, go on," she murmured and he felt her hips twisting as he traced down further, pressing gently into the slight convexity of her belly. Then he felt the wild, black, downy touch of her against him, and pressed his face deep into her Venus mound that had risen to meet him. Little gasps came from her as her hips twisted and lifted, her thighs opening, closing, then falling open again. "Please, please, please . . . yes, yes, yes," she called out, her hands clasping the back of his neck.

He slid down, letting his fingers press the inside of her thighs and felt the dampness of them, the nectar of eternal excitement. He moved further, lightly touching the edge of her warm, moist lips and Clea screamed, twisting and lifting, her hands now clutching tightly at him. He felt the urgency sweeping through her, and turned his torso to press against her, his own throbbing warmth against her dense, black thatch, then slid down, probing, and entering her, the little gasps now growing higher, stronger, flitting on the edge of a scream. She dug into the cot with her heels, almost flinging herself forward upon him and her whole body seemed caught up in a frenzy of touch. Hands, arms, legs, pubis, breasts—every part of her sliding, pulling, clutching, squeezing, twisting, and thrusting, as if she didn't want one inch where their bodies didn't touch, their skins didn't press together, their senses didn't absorb each other.

"More, more, more," she urged, the words torn from her as she lay against him, around him, under and atop him. Encompassed by her raging passions, he felt every twitching movement of her every pulsating, quivering contraction. She was a tempest of the senses, her intensity demanding the same of him as he felt himself swept up in her wildness, heard his own cries echoing hers, his thrusting pleasure spiraling to new heights. He felt her fingers digging into his sides as her gasped cries became screams. She flung her head back as her body arched upward to take in all of him, revel in every last inch, and her breasts quivering, her little fists beating against his shoulders.

"Now, now, now, oh, God, nooooowwwwww!" Clea screamed and he felt himself exploding with her. Clea's short hair bounced in rhythm with her breasts as her moment came, that instant of ecstasy always the same yet always new, that timeless instant of forever. She clung as she screamed until her cry suddenly broke off, and then her hands unclasped, trailing down his chest as she gave an anguished little sigh. But her legs stayed clasped around him, holding him inside of her in a sweet vise. "Stay, stay," she murmured, and he let himself relax in her warmth. Finally, with a resigned moan, her thighs fell open and her body grew limp, the flesh conceding the end of ecstasy.

He lay with her, one hand resting in her dense, black triangle and she sighed contentedly. Finally, she rose up on one elbow, her perky little breasts brushing across his chest. "I'm worried, Fargo," she said and he frowned at her.

"About what?" he queried.

"First, about the Comanche. I heard you talking to Matt Benton and Solita. My cousins were killed by the Comanche," she said.

"We could be lucky and avoid them," he said honestly.

"Then what about all those attempts to stop Solita's expedition? Unless you feel differently about them, now?" she asked almost hopefully.

"No, it all still doesn't fit right," he said.

"I'm just worried, mostly about Uncle Harry," Clea said. "He's not up to any more close calls like the one you rescued us from. He's not really all that well." Fargo listened with surprise. Harry Paxton had seemed quite healthy to him. "If there's any more trouble, would you try to see to Uncle Harry?" Clea asked. "I know it's a lot to ask but I've no one else to turn to."

"I'll do my best," he said and her lips pressed to his at once.

"Thank you, Fargo. I'll feel better just knowing that," she said.

He rose, swinging his long legs from the cot and started to pull on his trousers. "I'll be going, now, while everybody's still asleep. Nothing good will come out of gossip," he said.

"Absolutely not," Clea agreed. She reached over and picked up the short nightshirt. She started to pull it over her head, and had it half on when the tent flap pulled open and the candlelight fell on Solita's tall, slender shape.

"Don't you dare take that off," she snapped at Clea, words thrown out as if they were bullets.

Fargo saw Clea glance at him as they both instantly realized Solita's mistaken conclusion that they were about to engage in lovemaking. "She's the boss." He shrugged and Clea pulled the garment over her body. Solita's eyes were black with fury as they bored into Clea.

"I don't want to see you near him again like this, do you hear me?" Solita shot at Clea.

Fargo saw Clea's snub-nosed face grow tight. "I do what I want on my own time," she returned.

"While you're here, you're on *my* time. *I* make the rules around here. I find you trying this again, and you're out of here," Solita snapped.

"You need me," Clea said stubbornly.

"I need a cook. That's Harry Paxton," Solita corrected haughtily.

"He can't do it alone. He won't," Clea said stubbornly.

"Then you're both gone. I'll cook myself if I have to, but I won't have you doing any more of this. You'd better believe me, you little tramp," Solita flung viciously at her. Fargo watched the anger burning in Clea's face, but she didn't answer. He was glad to see that she had sense enough to know that Solita wasn't one for idle threats. Solita whirled toward the tent flap, halting to glare back at Fargo. "I'll see you outside," she said and stormed from the tent. Fargo finished pulling on clothes and saw Clea's satisfied little smile as he left the tent, a smile that said she was having the last laugh.

Outside, Fargo found Solita waiting a dozen yards from the tent and hurried to her. "You certainly made your point to her," he said.

"She's lucky," Solita hissed. "If I'd gotten here a few minutes later and found her screwing you she'd be out of here tonight. As for you, save her until after we've finished, if you still have a mind for her. I'm paying you to spend your every minute thinking about the trail, not her tail. Frankly, I expected more integrity and responsibility on your part."

"I didn't expect this kind of jealousy on yours," he said blandly.

Her eyes widened, flashed dark rage at him. "Jealousy? How ridiculous. How perfectly absurd."

"How true." He smiled.

"If you want to think that, go ahead, enjoy yourself. Just stay away from her or she's gone," Solita hissed and started to storm away.

"What brought you out looking?" he called.

She turned back. "I couldn't sleep and went for a walk. I saw your Ovaro and your bedroll, but not you. I suddenly had the thought."

"And you decided to go snooping," he said.

"I wanted to prove myself wrong," she said. "It seems I overestimated your taste as well as your discretion." As she strode away, Fargo smiled. He knew jealousy when he saw it. It always had its own kind of special fury. His smile stayed as he walked back to his bedroll. Solita's dark, sensuous fire could break out of its wall, he saw. But he also knew he couldn't let Clea pay the price for Solita's icy anger, not even if she wanted to be reckless. He had glimpsed that Clea had a hardheaded realism beneath her tomboy swagger. He'd see that she didn't lose sight of it. Reaching his bedroll, he stretched out and let sleep take over the remainder of the night.

Waking with the dawn, he was first in line at the chuck wagon as Harry Paxton brewed the morning coffee. "Clea told me she had hard words with Solita," Harry mentioned. "Said you were involved."

"She tell you why?" Fargo asked carefully.

"No, but I'm good at guessing and I know Clea," Harry said.

"I don't like being told what I can do and what I can't," Clea's voice cut in as she came from behind the wagon.

"You don't have to like it, you just have to do it," Harry said sharply as Clea glowered. "You know what this job means to us. Don't ruin it with your hot little temper, or your hot little anything else."

Clea's eyes went to Fargo. "Listen to your uncle." He smiled. "I'll be here when the job's finished."

"That helps," Clea said, her face softening. "That, and one other thing, the thing that Solita doesn't know about."

"Keep thinking about that," Fargo said, and finished his coffee and hurried away as Matt Benton and the others started to line up at the chuck wagon. He returned to the Ovaro and swung onto the horse as Solita came by. "Be back when you're ready to roll," he said. She nodded, her handsome face now composed, aloof, with no echo of the night's events. But then, he'd expected no less from her. She'd not let her feelings show, a controlled ability Clea would never have. He turned the Ovaro north and rode along the mountainside that formed the east wall of the Great Divide. His eyes searched for the passes he had traveled before, finally finding one wide enough to accommodate the wagons, and rode back to where Matt Benton had the wagons ready to roll.

He gave Benton directions and took another long look at the guards as they passed him riding behind the last of the wagons. When he spurred the pinto forward, Fargo's brow knitted as he uttered a silent prayer that the Comanche wouldn't find their scout for days and they'd just accept the fact when they did. After all, the sudden, unexpected encounter was part of life in the harsh ways of this rugged land. When he reached the pass, the wagons were following close behind and Solita came alongside him as he watched the wagons begin the climb. The pass curved, bordered by burr oak and juniper, growing steeper but the horses kept climbing, having to take frequent stops to rest in between. It was near the day's end when the procession reached the high flatland, with Albuquerque directly to the north.

They were headed toward Albuquerque when Fargo drew up beside Solita. "Albuquerque is a fairsized town, now. They're not going to look kindly on your digging up their streets and buildings," he said.

"I won't have to. Written accounts say they didn't stop at Albuquerque proper. They stopped just north of it," she said.

"North is a big place," Fargo said.

"Maybe not that big," she said, rummaging through one of the sacks on the packhorse and bringing out a battered little pad of paper bound together with string. "A piece of writing from one of Coronado's soldiers who made it back alive," Solita said. "He writes that where they chased the Aztecs was a place of the *sangre de drago*, the blood of the dragon, of spiderwebs without spiders, a place of a thousand green sunbursts. It had no name, then."

Fargo's eyes narrowed in thought as he turned Solita's words in his mind. "Let's keep going," he said and led the way around Albuquerque, avoiding the sprawling, crowded town. When they had bypassed the town, he kept north, his eyes sweeping the land on all sides until he suddenly reined to a halt. He scanned the large stretch of terrain directly in front of him and a speculative smile edged his lips as he took in the array of vegetation. He saw Ajo oak, piñon pine, alligator juniper, switch sorrel, and red-berry buckthorn, but his eyes kept returning to where three other, very unusual shrubs and bushes grew in profusion. "There." He nodded. "They made camp somewhere in that area."

"How do you know?" Solita said, dismounting with him. She followed as he walked first to a large expanse of scraggly, gray-green shrubs. "Limber bush," he said, kneeling down on one knee to snap one of the stems in two. Sap ran out at once, a reddish hued liquid. "*Sangre de drago*," he said. "The Spanish for the Indian name. The Indians used the red sap as a dye." He walked on to the tall, wavy spires of the ocotillo shrubs. Hundreds of thin, spidery spikes jutted out from each wavy spire to give the shrubs a cobwebbed effect.

"Spiders without webs," Solita breathed and he nodded, then steered her to where the big sotol plants grew. Their thin, long, vibrant green fronds exploded in every direction. "A thousand green sunbursts," Solita said.

"Start digging," he said and she hurried to where her crew of diggers waited. They quickly began to break ground under her direction while they still had daylight. As they began to work, Fargo made another list of the plants, animals, and birds he had spotted in the area, then pushed it into his pocket and paused beside the Ovaro as one of the diggers called out. He followed Solita to where they presented her two skeletons still encased in armored breastplates and helmets. Halberds, gisarmes, daggers, and two crossbows were found near the skeletons, along with deerskin water pouches in surprisingly good condition. Solita directed the retrieval and the careful wrapping of all the items as darkness began to blanket the land.

"They'll keep digging in the morning," she said, but he saw no elation in her face.

"Expected you'd be happier," Fargo said. "They're finding plenty of items for you to bring back to the university."

"Yes, of course I'm pleased," she said, but her face didn't reflect her answer as she hurried away. Night descended and he went to the chuck wagon to get some supper. Clea found a moment to press herself against him for a fleeting moment.

"Wouldn't want you to forget," she murmured.

"Not much chance of that," he told her. Later, stretched out on his bedroll, Fargo found himself thinking about Solita. He hadn't mistaken the disappointment in her face at the digging and that, too, didn't fit. She was continuing to find real evidence of Coronado's route and pursuit of the Aztecs, the sole purpose of the expedition, according to her. There was no reason for disappointment. It had been fleeting, yet very real. She remained a puzzle, not unlike a beautiful picture slightly out of focus, where nothing was exactly as it ought to be. He finally slept but thoughts of Solita clung to the edges of his thoughts, faintly irritating him.

When morning came, the diggers found more artifacts and a number of Aztec weapons and beads. Again, Fargo looked for satisfaction if not enthusiasm in Solita's face and found neither. He took the Ovaro and rode west into the Cebolleta Mountains, his lips drawn back, his thoughts on the Comanche. If they were coming, this is where they'd be—high enough to see and not be seen from below. Fargo sent the pinto through a narrow rock passage, found a high perch, and moved out onto it. He scanned the mostly rocky mountain paths, interspersed with a few clusters of piñon pine and sycamore. He made a note of a flight of juncos that took wing, and picked out a small herd of feral burros, as well as a coatimundi that emerged from a high rock. But there was no other movement in the mountains, and he was about to turn and go back down the mountainside when a horseman suddenly appeared, moving slowly from behind a line of tall rocks.

Moving onto a narrow ledge, the horseman was followed by another, then another until Fargo watched

161

eight Comanche spread across the ledge. They took up different positions that let them see anything that moved anywhere below. Fargo cursed softly. They had found their scout, but they hadn't been content to leave it at that as he had hoped they would. The rest was easy enough to put together. They'd gone down into the divide, seen the wagon tracks, and followed them. Now they'd wait to see more before they decided on their next move. He backed the pinto from the ledge, staying in the rocky passages as he made his way down the mountainside, emerging on the flatland below. They'd see him instantly there, he knew, but they'd not do anything more than watch. They were waiting to see more. The Comanche knew the value of patience.

Putting the pinto into a slow canter, he returned to Solita and the crew. The diggers were finished, the wagons loaded and ready to move. "My maps tell me they made two side trips not far from here, one to Taos, the other to the place you call Las Vegas," Solita said. "The maps tell me exactly where they are. We'll take Taos, first." Fargo moved to the head of the wagons and led the way northwest. It was a long, dry haul, skirting the Ponderosa Mountains, and it was almost dark when they reached the spot Solita's map indicated just south of Taos. Fargo had ridden with his eyes scanning the land behind them as much as he had on the trail ahead.

"What are you looking for?" Solita asked him at the end of the day.

"Comanche," he said. "They've seen us, and watched what we were doing. I'd wager they're following us."

"You're still worried about them," she mused.

"That's an understatement," he said. "Guess I'm still an unbeliever."

She returned a tolerantly amused smile. "You'll see," she said.

"Honey, you don't know how much I hope you're right," he said. As dark descended, they pulled the wagons into a half circle. He felt the same weariness as everyone else, and was happy to set out his bedroll beyond the campsite. He had just finished when Matt Benton came to him.

"Solita told me you think the Comanche are following us," he said. "I'm going to set out sentries for the night, in four-hour shifts."

"No," Fargo said and Benton's face started to protest. "Unless you just want to lose some men," Fargo said quickly. "First, like most Indians, the Comanche don't much like night fighting, but they do like picking off sentries. It's one of their favorite things to do. Second, if they were going to attack us, they'd have done so long ago. There were plenty of spots to do it. No, they're still waiting, watching, wondering what we're doing. You don't need sentries tonight, not yet."

Matt Benton gave a reluctant shrug. "Hope you know what you're doing," he grumbled as he walked away.

"I do," Fargo said and silently hoped he did himself. Alone, he stretched out on the bedroll and pulled sleep around himself. He didn't know exactly how long he'd slept when his innate instincts snapped him awake. The Colt instantly in his hand, he rose up on one elbow and peered into the night catching the dark shadow of movement inside the branches of a sycamore. He glimpsed a slender, tall form disappearing into the shadows. He smiled as the moment vanished and he lay back and let sleep come to him again. When morning came, he rose to find the diggers already at work, Solita standing by, supervising closely. He sidled up to her. "Couldn't sleep again last night? Or just doing a little checking up?" he murmured.

"You must try not letting your imagination run off with you," she said with a kind of deprecating hauteur. He let his smile show that he dismissed her answer as she turned her attention back to the digging. The morning was half over when she came to him. "Just more of the same," she said crossly. "We'll go on to Las Vegas. My map says they stopped there as well. You'll take us there quickly—I want to make up time."

"Can't promise that, not in this climate. But we've been through that," he said.

"Do your best," she snapped and stalked away. He waited until the artifacts discovered were safely in the wagons and then led the way southeast, staying along the Coyote River as long as he could before turning south toward Las Vegas. During a pause to let the horses drink, Solita showed him the map, where a little collection of scraggly lines pinpointed a spot just east of Las Vegas. But the night arrived at the spot at the same time the wagons did. "Damn," he heard Solita hiss angrily.

"You on a schedule?" Fargo asked with an edge in his voice.

"Yes," she snapped. "My own." Her eyes shot daggers at him as she took her horses aside. Her patience was growing thinner, he decided and again he wondered why. He found a spot at the edge of a stand of piñon pine and unsaddled the Ovaro. It had been a dry, hot trip and he'd driven everyone as hard as he dared to. The camp settled quickly to sleep. Fargo, on his bedroll, was almost asleep himself when he heard the sound of soft footsteps. No tall, slender shape this time, but a smallish, rounded figure coming toward him in a short nightdress.

"What are you doing here?" Fargo asked, sitting up.

"What do you think?" Clea returned tartly.

"I think you're acting crazy and you'd better get away from here," he said sternly.

Clea knelt down with him. "She was up snooping around last night. I saw her. She won't do it again tonight," Clea said.

He started to push her from the bedroll. "That's exactly the kind of thinking that'll get you in big trouble. It's called underestimating your opponent," he said.

"You really think that?" Clea frowned.

"I sure as hell do. I'm only thinking about you. She meant every word she said," he told her severely. Clea pouted back, pressing her round, high breasts against his chest, but then pushed to her feet when she got no response. "Good girl," he said and she hurried away, still pouting. He watched her run off, settled back onto the bedroll and lay awake for a spell longer. But no other fleeting forms appeared and he went to sleep. When morning came, Solita had the diggers hard at work. They recovered a few more artifacts, and he saw more angry impatience in Solita's regal face.

"We'll press on," she said to Fargo. "Their trail went east into Texas territory, near Pampas." She showed him the primitive map again.

"You can start on your own," he said and pointed off in one direction. "Head straight that way," he said.

"Where are you going?" Solita questioned sharply.

"To see if we still have company," he answered.

"Hurry back. I want you leading us," Solita ordered and he swung onto the pinto and rode past Matt Benton and the wagons as they prepared to move on. He stayed south and his eyes swept the land as he rode, probing every rock formation, every uprising of red granite stone, carefully searching the vast expanse of flatland and the giant saguaros that dotted the landscape, each plenty large enough to hide a man. He was in the flatlands when he spied the first rider, a lone figure. But then he expected that the Comanche wouldn't ride together. It wasn't their way when they were trailing someone. He hung back, carefully glancing all around and finally, one by one, he found the others.

Each rode alone but at the same pace as the others as they spread across the edge of the distant land. A furrow creased Fargo's brow. There were only six—two were missing. His jaw set firm, he turned the pinto and rode back the way he'd come. He caught up to the wagons along the Ute River, finding Solita beside Matt Benton. "You took long enough," she said reproachfully.

"We still have company?" Benton asked.

"Two less," Fargo bit out.

"They giving up?" Benton asked.

"Just the opposite, dammit. They sent two back for their main force," Fargo said. "They'll be coming back, this time for real."

"Maybe we'll be finished by then," Solita put in. "In any case, I'm not worried."

"The power of believing," Fargo said.

"The power of what we don't want to believe," she corrected. "A place of betrayal, remember? Come now, your memory isn't that short, Fargo."

He swore under his breath as he sent the pinto forward, taking the lead as they crossed the river and pressed forward. It was nearing the day's end when they moved into Texas territory, and they halted by a large stand of hackberry beside a pond. As the others made camp, Fargo rode back the way they had come, his eyes slowing searching the terrain until night fell. Camp was already a silent and sleeping place when he reached it, except for the chuck wagon, where Harry Paxton had just finished washing off tin plates.

He had enough stew left to give Fargo a plate, and Clea appeared to sit beside him.

"You rode back looking for Comanche," she said and he nodded. "See any?"

"No, but they'll be coming," he answered.

"Benton says you make too much out of the Comanche," Clea said.

"There are those who make too little about the Comanche. You know where they are? They're all dead," Fargo said and Clea fell silent until he finished his meal.

"Thanks for caring," she said as she brushed his lips in a quick kiss.

"It's not all selfless. It's my neck, too," Fargo told her as he walked away leading the pinto. He found a spot near the far edge of the pond and bedded down. He woke early to see Solita just returning from the pond, her jet black hair still wet, little droplets of water alighting on her skin, the top of her damp blouse hanging open. He watched her golden glow as the new sun caught her skin, lending her an almost translucent quality. She noticed him staring after a moment and pulled her blouse closed. "Modesty must be served," he remarked.

Her eyes held his for a moment but she kept her face blank. "I want to reach Pampas by noon," she said.

"That's asking a lot," he said.

"Not if you stop babying the horses and the equipment," she said, her voice made of ice.

"What's your hurry?" he asked.

"I've my reasons," she said.

"Why do I feel they're not worth a damn," he bit out.

"That's not fair," she protested.

"And that's no answer," he said.

"It'll have to do," she snapped, not giving an inch.

He climbed onto the pinto. "We'll do it my way, in my time," he said. She glared back but didn't answer as she strode away. Fargo motioned to Matt Benton to start the wagons, and turned the pinto and started out ahead. Riding at an easy pace, he scanned the mostly flatland dotted with giant saguaros, creosote shrubs, and increasingly larger stands of hackberry. Every so often, he'd drop back and check the land at their backtrail, but each time he saw no signs of the Comanche, and returned to lead the procession. They reached Pampas not long after noon and Solita produced her map with the exact spot already marked. It was surprisingly accurate, and Solita had the diggers quickly at work.

She came to Fargo as he relaxed under a gambel oak, lowering herself down beside him, her long, supple body moving smoothly as a willow wand. "I'm sorry I was so short-tempered before," she said and he laughed. "Did I say something funny?" she asked coolly.

"Yes. You can even make an apology sound like a command," he said. "I think you need more practice."

"At what?"

"Apologizing," he said.

She thought for a moment and looked beautifully

serious. "Perhaps. I've not done it often," she said, and the way she said it made him suddenly feel sorry for her, as though she had recognized a piece of her upbringing was missing. She rose and returned to the digging until it was finished. He was standing beside the Ovaro when she came back, anger in her face. "Not enough of anything," she muttered. "We'll go north, cross the Oklahoma territory into Kansas and on to Wichita."

"We'll start in the morning, give everybody a good rest tonight," Fargo said.

"We'll start now, and get in another two hours before night," Solita said. He studied her for a moment. She wasn't simply being callous and arbitrary, he decided. Something was eating at her, something out of place, something he'd still try and understand, he promised himself as he swung into the saddle and began to lead the way directly north. When night fell, they made camp in the narrow sliver of land that was north Oklahoma, sandwiched between Texas and Kansas. Matt Benton sat down to eat with him.

"The men think the Comanche should have caught up to us by now. We've been making some turns and twists. They're guessing the Comanche have lost our trail," Benton said.

"The Comanche wouldn't lose a rabbit trail, much less wagon tracks," Fargo said.

"Then why haven't they caught up?" Benton asked.

"Who says they haven't?" Fargo returned and drew a frown from Benton. "Your men have been looking over their shoulders all day, wondering, waiting, looking, getting more and more nervous as they didn't see a single Comanche. That's part of the Comanche tactics. Like the hawk knows how to make the rabbit run, the Comanche know how to make a man sweat, and get so nervous he can't shoot straight."

Benton said nothing for a long moment. "Since you're so sure they're coming, what do you figure to do when they get here?"

"I won't know that till they show," Fargo said.

"You think we've any chance?" Benton asked.

"Nobody's unbeatable," Fargo said, then rose and took his plate to the wreck pan before he stretched out on his bedroll. The answer he'd given to Matt Benton haunted him; *nobody's unbeatable*. It wasn't untrue. You just had to know how to do it. And that was a lot harder than words.

10

The morning dawned hot, the sun quickly flooding the land. Breakfast was over, the coffee and biscuits consumed, the horses were hitched and the wagons were ready to roll when the shout cut through the quiet murmur. Fargo instantly heard the edge of panic in it, and he turned to see one of Matt Benton's guards at the rear of the wagons waving an arm. Swinging onto the Ovaro, Fargo rode back to the man and instantly saw the reason for the man's agitation. A double row of horsemen were lined up some thousand yards away, barechested on their short-legged pintos and quarter horse stock Indian ponies. They sat motionless as Fargo edged out, keeping the Ovaro at a walk as he approached the Comanche.

He finally halted some five hundred yards from them, letting his eyes roam across the double row as he quickly counted. "Fifty," he breathed and grimaced. He had already made a count of Solita's crew—twelve guards, eight diggers, six drivers. With Matt Benton, Harry and Clea and Solita, that made thirty in all, not counting himself. The best of them were only average shots, Fargo was certain, and he winced again, focusing on the Comanche at the center of the first line. The Indian sat on an almost all-white pony with a brown patch on one side of its head. Tall and lean, the Comanche wore a lone eagle's feather in his long, black hair. A golden amulet on a rawhide necklace rested on his chest and Fargo took in his flat-cheekboned face, his thin, beaked nose giving him the appearance of a peregrine falcon. His manner and bearing marked him as the chief, even without the eagle feather.

Turning, Fargo slowly rode back to the wagons, aware that everyone's eyes were on him as he re-joined the procession. "Let's roll. We're moving out," he said.

"That's all?" Matt Benton frowned.

"For now," Fargo said.

"They could charge us any time," Matt said.

"They won't," Fargo said and Solita caught up to him as he rode forward. She stayed silent, aware that he was immersed in his own thoughts. For his part, Fargo was aware of her beside him but his mind stayed absorbed turning over one plan after another. Just a little over an hour had passed when Matt Benton paid his first visit of the morning.

"They're just following, staying plenty far back, but following," Benton said. "The men are all getting nervous."

"That's exactly what the Comanche want. They're counting on it. Tell your men to stay calm, and to keep riding as usual," Fargo said and Benton left, his face still wreathed in concern. Fargo glanced at Solita, seeing a total lack of concern in her face. The Aztec fetish she believed in had a firm hold on her. But then his certainties had an equally firm hold on him. In this standoff, he wouldn't object if she was right, he admitted. Matt Benton's second visit came an hour later.

"The men are getting really bothered," Matt said. "Wondering and listening and looking back—it's all getting to them."

"You too?" Fargo queried.

Benton's shrug was its own admission. "The men feel we ought to make a stand, get ready before they come at us," Benton said.

"Tell them we make a stand at the right place and the right time. Anything else won't be a stand. It'll be stopping to commit suicide," Fargo said and Benton again returned to the wagons. Fargo held to the same, steady pace. The Comanche were certain they could reduce their quarry to such frenzied nervousness they'd be easy targets, and he swore at their understanding of human weaknesses. But perhaps their tactics could be turned back on them, he pondered. His eyes scanned the land and realized that the saguaros had almost ceased dotting the terrain, and the creosote bushes had given way to grama grass. They had crossed into Kansas. As the sun began to sink toward the horizon, he rode back to Matt Benton and sent him east toward the Red Hills. As the wagons changed direction, Fargo rode to the rear and watched the distant line of Comanche as they shifted directions to follow the wagons.

He let a satisfied grunt pass his lips. The Comanche were still content to play their game of nerves. They hadn't figured out yet where he was going. Now time had shifted to their advantage, Fargo knew. He turned the pinto and hurried forward to rejoin the wagons, pausing beside Matt Benton. "When I give the word, send those wagons as fast and as hard as you can," he said and Benton nodded gravely. Riding on, Fargo passed Solita, seeing the little furrow of curiosity touch her brow. Fargo peered ahead through the slanting rays of the late afternoon sun, his gaze sweeping the land ahead.

He rode perhaps another hour, the sun now starting to touch the horizon, when he saw the Red Hills come into view, rising up from the flat plains. He held back another fifteen minutes. Timing was paramount. He needed enough daylight left to let him find the right spot, and just enough time for the shielding curtain of darkness to descend. Slowing, he let the wagons catch up to him, then rose in the saddle and shouted back to Matt Benton. "Now!" he shouted. "Follow me!" He paused for Matt to pass on the command, and saw the wagons start to gather speed before sending the Ovaro into a gallop. He led the way through a wide opening in the hills, his eyes searching both sides of the terrain, passing stands of gambel oak and hack-berry, checking over the shape of the rocks, the curves and slopes of the hills.

The Comanche would be putting their ponies into a gallop, now, recovering from their surprise and quickly alarmed by the unexpected flight of the wagons. But they had lost precious minutes and were still far enough back. They still had time on his side, Fargo told himself as he steered the wagons into the hills as fast as the terrain would allow. His eyes swept the hills, discarding anyplace with overhanging ledges and trees too close to the rocks. His lips were drawn back in a grimace as precious seconds slipped by, when suddenly he spotted what he wanted—a wall of sandstone not too high with an expanse of open land in front of it.

He turned and raced to the spot and the others followed. "Make a half circle with the rocks at your backs. One wagon at each end, tight against the rocks, the others forming the half circle, with the chuck wagon in the middle," he said and rode back and forth, directing the drivers in positioning their wagons. When he finished, the half circle was complete, the wall of rocks an impenetrable backdrop. "Unhitch the horses, and close the wagons against each other end to end," he ordered and dismounted to help finish the job. He turned to Solita. "You told me you had plenty of extra rifles. Everyone gets one now—diggers, drivers, everybody," he said. She nodded and with Benton beside her, broke out a box of the extra rifles and handed them around. They had just finished when the Comanche rode into sight, barely visible in the deep dusk as they halted and surveyed the wagons.

As dusk became dark, they moved back from sight. "They won't attack till morning," Fargo told the others. "I'll spell out exactly what I want you to do before then. Meanwhile, relax and get some shut-eye. We'll post sentries in four-hour shifts, just in case they send some buck to sacrifice himself. But I doubt that. It's not the Comanche way. Sioux, Cheyenne, or Crow, maybe, but not Cheyenne." As Benton began to choose the sentries, Fargo walked over to the chuck wagon where Clea and Harry Paxton looked on.

"I don't care what she sees anymore," Clea muttered, approaching Fargo to embrace him.

"I do. Step back, girl," her uncle ordered and Clea obeyed.

"Each man gets a cup of coffee a half hour before dawn," Fargo told Paxton. "You can brew coffee in the dark, I hope."

"Been doing it for years," Harry replied. "You don't want me making a fire for supper, I guess."

"No. I'd say most of the men haven't any hankering for supper anyway. A man doesn't have much appetite with his stomach in knots," Fargo said and began a slow walk around the half circle of wagons. He made mental notes, formed plans, tried to anticipate the unexpected, and finally felt satisfied that he'd worked out everything he had considered the best they could. He stretched out atop his bedroll and saw Solita nearby on a blanket, already asleep. He found himself admiring the inner peace that believing in the power of unknown forces could bring, and Fargo managed to get in a few hours of fitful sleep. His inner alarm clock set, he awoke an hour before dawn, and started to move among the men and found only a few that needed waking. Solita knelt at the outside of the circle that surrounded him.

"I've worked out a plan. It's your blueprint for staying alive. It can work if you stick to it. That means you can't let the Comanche trigger you into doing what they want you to do," Fargo began.

"What's that?" some asked.

"Let your instincts make you do the wrong thing. Make you fight on their terms. That means you've got to stay disciplined. You've got to make the Comanche fight on your terms."

"How do we do that?" someone else questioned.

"By sticking to the blueprint I'll give you, no matter what," Fargo said. "I'll spell it out for each of you. Stick to it, focus on your assignments, and we can win. It all hangs on one thing. The Comanche have their way of fighting. Interrupt that, and they can be beaten. Surprise them, confuse them, knock them off stride, and you will win. But you have to know what to expect. The first thing the Comanche will do is pour bullets and arrows into you. They'll make a ferocious show of it and they'll be fast-moving targets you'll never hit unless you're all sharpshooters."

"We sure ain't that," someone snorted.

"That's why you can't fight their fight. That'll be suicide. Their first attack will be designed to scare the hell out of you and make you fire back in an instinctive reaction. That'll tell them where you are. Then they'll really come at you."

"We'll have to fire back sooner or later," Matt Benton said.

"Only when we're ready, when we can do the most damage," Fargo said and followed by giving each man detailed instructions as Harry and Clea distributed coffee. It was almost dawn when he finished, but most everyone had been assigned a place and told what to do and when to do it. Fargo watched the men break up and find their places, most remaining close by the wagons. He saw Solita come toward him.

"You left me out," she said. "It so happens I can probably outshoot anyone here, except you."

"I didn't leave you out. I just kept you for last," Fargo told her. "You'll stay with me. I'll be sharpshooting, following trouble spots. I'll be moving around but I can't be in two places at once. That's where you'll come in."

She gave a satisfied nod and stayed with Fargo as he scanned the figures flattened down behind the half circle of wagons. The sun edged over the top of the hills and he saw why they were named the Red Hills, as the sandstone took on a reddish hue in the waning sunlight. With the big Henry clutched in one hand, Fargo moved to a spot beside the chuck wagon, the tallest of the wagons that butted against each other. Clea and Harry positioned themselves halfway down the left half of the wagons. Solita lowered herself beside Fargo, her rifle in the crook of one arm. Listening, Fargo picked up the faint sound of the hooves of unshod ponies moving slowly forward. He strained his ears and a grim smile touched his lips. They were coming in from both ends of the hills. It was a clever tactic, and he hoped the men would keep their self-discipline. That's what worried him most, Fargo realized. Without steady nerves, his plan would come apart.

The hoofbeats suddenly ceased. There was a moment of utter silence, and then the world seemed to explode in pounding hooves and high-pitched screams. They came in from both ends, racing their ponies at full speed as they screamed and hollered, galloping back and forth in front of the half circle of wagons. Their war whoops were accompanied by the staccato sounds of rifle fire and whistling arrows. Fargo, flattened behind one of the wagons with Solita at his side, listened to the thudding, splintering, cracking sounds of bullets and arrows hitting wood and earth. Then, as suddenly as it had begun, the first attack ceased and there was a moment of strange calm. Fargo allowed a grunt of approval to drop from his lips. Benton's men had held fast. Not a sound had come from the wagons.

Fargo peeked out at the Comanche from beneath the wagon. They were milling back and forth and he saw their chief, the gold amulet glinting upon his chest, bring his arm forward in a short, chopping motion. His braves sent their ponies racing back to attack again. This time they came in closer to the wagons, again filling the air with bullets and arrows. But again, there was no answering fire as they raced back and forth. With Benton and the others hidden from sight as they lay behind the wagons, the Comanche had to wonder if there was anyone there. They charged again and came still closer, and when they were met once again with only silence from the wagons, they raced their ponies in real close, shooting arrows in arcs that dropped them onto the ground in back of the wagons. But there was still no answering fire, and as the Comanche came in even closer, Fargo decided they were near enough for even the worst of Benton's marksmen to hit their targets.

He pushed to his feet and began firing at the Comanche, bringing down two almost at once. It was the signal the rest of the crew waited upon. Benton and the others rolled out from behind the wagons, got to their feet, and began firing, sending a hail of lead at the surprised Comanche. Fargo saw the unexpected barrage of bullets take a toll beyond his expectations as Comanche warriors were blasted from their ponies before they could wheel around to race away. Fargo guessed that at least a quarter of the attackers went down in that first, close-up barrage. He brought down three with rapid-fire precision, using the big Henry. But as the rest of the Comanche raced back to their chief, the inaccurate marksmanship of Benton's defenders was instantly apparent. They were unable to hit any of the attackers as they raced away.

It was a fact the Comanche would immediately note, Fargo cursed. Moreover, they now knew where the defenders had been hiding. His mouth curled in a frown, he watched the Indians regroup for a change in tactics. They had been hurt, but they had more than enough warriors left to strike again, and strike hard. Stepping back a few paces, Fargo called out to the others waiting by the wagons. "Special squads get ready. Stick to your assignments, no matter what. I'll be backing you up," he reiterated and stepped back to where Solita waited. "You ready?" he asked her, and she nodded. He spotted the Comanche as they conferred with their chief. Fargo hoped he had guessed right about what they'd do next.

Though the wagons were against each other end-to-end, the fit was not air-tight. Wagon shafts and variations in wagon height and wheel size prevented that. There was enough space for any good horse to jump through the wagon line where they butted each other. That's exactly what he expected the Comanche to do next. They'd not present any more easy targets, now that they knew the defenders were poor shots. But he had set up the special squads to nullify the tactic, their assignment to focus on the riders that vaulted over the wagons. Sudden shouts from the Comanche broke off his thoughts and he saw the Comanche again racing for the wagons. But they did not race back and forth this time. They broke off into smaller groups and charged directly at the wagons.

Fargo watched as the first group of attackers leaped over the gap between the wagons, landing behind the defenders. But he was glad to see his special squads hold to their assignments, bringing down the Comanche warriors as their ponies hit the ground. Fargo grunted in satisfaction. He had guessed right about the Comanche tactics. Then, with shattering suddenness, his guess exploded in his face. The second wave of Comanche attackers didn't jump their ponies between the wagons. Rather, they dropped from their horses at the last moment and climbed onto the wagons on foot as a third wave again jumped their ponies. He then saw a fourth wave drop from their mounts, joining the attack on foot. They were too small and too fast-moving a target for Benton's men as they lay down a fast, withering fire.

Fargo saw Benton's men begin to fall. Worse still, the special squads he had set up lost their concentration. They began to fire at the Comanche on foot who climbed over the wagons, as more warriors leaped the gaps to land behind the defenders. Fargo swore bitterly. He had guessed right only to have the Comanche's own tactical shrewdness outfox him. He spun and dropped to one knee with Solita beside him. "Pick a target, any Comanche anywhere," he said as he took down three of the attackers. Solita took down two. He turned and saw a Comanche about to leap from the top of a wagon at her and fired. The Indian landed almost at her feet. Sensing another figure behind him, Fargo whirled and saw a warrior leaping from the wagon at him, tomahawk raised.

Fargo had time only to bring the rifle around and use the thick stock to parry the blow. But the force of the strike still sent Fargo sprawling and as he landed on his back, the Comanche leaped at him, tomahawk still poised to strike. Fargo rolled as the man's weapon came down with brutal force, the axe digging into the ground a fraction of an inch from his head. There was neither time nor room to bring the rifle around, but Fargo had a split second to yank the Colt from its holster as the Indian pulled the tomahawk out of the ground. He shot the moment the gun cleared the holster, just as the Comanche raised the axe to strike again. The man's abdomen seemed to implode as the bullet slammed into him at point-blank range. His body curved inward as he fell away, the tomahawk dropping from his hand. Fargo scuttled backward and looked up to see Solita on one knee, firing into a knot of her diggers and some Comanche, in close hand-to-hand combat.

He also saw another Comanche atop one of the wagons drawing his bow back, his arrow aimed at Solita. Fargo fired and both bow and arrow flew from the man's hand as he toppled from the wagon. Fargo brought the rifle around and fired two quick shots as another Comanche dropped. Some of Benton's men came forward firing wildly but profusely, their erratic fire nonetheless taking a toll on the attackers. Fargo joined in with the big Henry when he heard a series of high-pitched calls from outside the circle of wagons. He saw the Comanche on foot slide and crawl from the wagons as they left, those still on their ponies leaping back between the wagons the way they had entered.

Fargo ran to one of the wagons, peering out to see the Comanche racing toward their chief. A quick count told him that they had lost more than half of their force and as he watched, the Comanche chief's falconish face lost none of its icy pride as he stared back defiantly at the wagons. His stare locked on the wagons, a piercing, fierce glare as his braves waited beside him. "What's this mean?" Matt Benton asked as he and the others looked on. Fargo's lake blue eyes met the chief's fierce stare.

"They're waiting for their dead," Fargo said. "Carry them outside. They'll collect them."

"You heard him. Get to it," Benton said. The chuck wagon was moved enough to widen a space as the slain Comanche were carried out. When the task was done, the chuck wagon was pushed back into place. Fargo climbed onto one of the wagons and watched as the Comanche carried their dead away on their ponies. He brought the rifle up as the Comanche chief rode forward alone, watching closely as the Indian raised his bow. He shot an arrow into the ground, where it stood high, its shaft and feathers quivering. With a last, piercing stare at Fargo, the Comanche chief slowly rode away, his warriors following him.

Fargo jumped down from the wagon when they disappeared into the hills. Benton and the others gathered around him. "Does that mean they're giving up, that they admit they lost?" Benton asked.

"Just the opposite. It means they admit a standoff but nothing else. They'll take their dead back to their burial grounds," Fargo said.

"Will they come at us again?" one of the guards asked.

"They could. Probably not right away, though," Fargo said. "How many did we lose?"

"They hit us hard once they got inside," Benton said. "We lost four diggers, five guards and three drivers, twelve altogether. We've got five wounded."

"Some of you tend to the wounded. The rest come

with me. We'll pick a place in the hills for burying our own dead. It's the best we can do," Fargo said.

"It's as good a place as any," Solita put in, her tone more matter-of-fact than sympathetic. "Get on with it," she ordered brusquely.

Fargo led the way with the burial party, and found a spot in a shady hollow in the hills and stood watch as the task was slowly completed. It was late afternoon when they finished, and on their way back Fargo found a small stream that meandered down near to where the wagons were still in place. Clea stood with Harry Paxton and a few others, tending to the wounded when Fargo arrived back at the wagons. "We need more water to clean wounds," she said.

"Take six men and all the canteens," he said and brought her to the stream, where every canteen was filled. They trudged back to the wagons.

"We could get in at least an hour's traveling," Solita said to him.

"Your crew need time to recover," Fargo said, not hiding the irritation in his voice. "They stay holed up here till morning."

She studied his annoyance. "You've got another reason for keeping us here," she said and he swore at her acuity.

"I don't need another. One'll do," he snapped and strode away. Harry Paxton left the wounded to Clea and the others, and cooked up a makeshift meal of beans. Everyone was too drained to eat dinner, anyway, and the meal was taken largely in silence. When it was over, the camp quickly fell to sleep. Fargo stood beside one of the wagons and peered out into the hills, turning when he saw the tall, willowy figure walking toward him.

"What is wrong?" Solita asked. "It's over. I told you they wouldn't win."

"Because of your fetish?" he snorted.

"Was I wrong?" she returned smugly.

He wanted to scoff at her and found he couldn't. Instead, he became defensive, and he hated himself for it. "I'd like to think my tactics had something to do with it," he grumbled.

"They did," she said. "And my fetish affected what you planned and did. You still don't understand how the power works."

"Guess not," he muttered.

"And you're still looking out into the night," she said.

"The Comanche don't take to going back home as losers, bringing only their dead. They'll want some way to save face. That's important to them," Fargo said.

"They've left," she said, dismissing his concerns. "It's over. Tomorrow we head for Wichita. I'll show you what my map says come morning."

"Your men could stand some more rest. They're not professional soldiers."

"No more rest. They go on. That's what they've been paid for. We've lost enough time," Solita said, the harshness sweeping through her instantly. Once more, Fargo wondered at the terrible urgency that consumed her. She strode away and he took his bedroll and slept heavily through the night.

Morning finally came, and he had just finished dressing when he heard Harry Paxton's voice, wrapped in alarm and fear. "Something's wrong, dammit . . . something's terribly wrong," the man called out.

"What's the matter?" Fargo asked, walking over to where Harry Paxton stood beside the chuck wagon.

"It's Clea. She's gone," Harry said.

"What do you mean *gone*?" Fargo frowned.

"I mean, gone, left," the man said.

"How do you know?"

"The big bucket is missing, the one we fill with water for making coffee. She must've taken it to get water at the stream. But she didn't come back." Harry Paxton said, worry edging his words.

"When did she take it?" Fargo asked.

"Had to be during the night sometime. She always hangs that short nightgown of hers on this here hook," Paxton said, gesturing to a wooden peg at the side of the wagon. "It's not here. That means she's still in it."

"Damned fool girl," Fargo bit out as he swung onto the Ovaro and sent the horse into a gallop, leaping the space between two of the wagons with a high vault. "I'll be back," he called over his shoulder as he raced away. The stream wasn't very far away and he was there in less than a minute. His heart sank when the first thing he saw turned out to be the bucket lying on its side. Jumping to the ground, he quickly found two sets of moccasined footprints and several unshod pony prints. "Damn," he swore as he climbed onto the horse and returned to the wagons. He felt Solita's eyes burning into him as he halted beside Harry and tossed the bucket on the ground.

"Oh my God," Harry groaned.

"The Comanche took her. They were still watching us," Fargo said. "She gave them what they wanted—a way to save face. They'll parade her around camp before they enjoy her."

"Good God," Harry Paxton groaned again. "Silly, impatient girl."

"I'll go after her," Fargo said. "Can't promise anything, but I'll try to bring her back."

"No." The single word cut in sharply, Solita's voice hard as steel. "She was a fool, and fools pay for their mistakes. It's as simple as that."

"Come out here with me," Fargo said as he rode out beyond the others' hearing range. Solita followed, her visage stolid and frosty as she halted beside him. "I'm giving you a chance not to show what a fourteen-carat bitch you can be," he said.

"I couldn't care less what they think I am. I care about reaching Wichita. You've been paid to help me. I expect you to live up to your agreement. That comes first," Solita threw at him.

"Sorry, honey. Doing what I think is right comes first," he replied.

"You told me the Comanche wanted to do something in order to save face. Now they have it. That means they'll leave us alone. Take that away from them and they could come at us madder than ever," Solita said.

He wanted to reject the truth of her logic but realized it was no time for lies. "Or they could give up, take it as a sign to go their own way and leave us be. I'll take that chance," he said.

"And if you get yourself killed?" she pressed.

"I don't plan on that," Fargo said.

"But it could happen. What then?"

"We'll both come up short, especially me," he said.

"This isn't fair. You owe me. We had an agreement," she insisted.

"And I'm not turning my back on Clea without trying," he said. "I'm finished talking." He turned the Ovaro and put the horse into a gallop, feeling Solita's dark eyes boring into his back as he rode off. Fargo wondered if she'd wait or try to go on herself. He tossed away the question to concentrate on searching the ground ahead.

11

Picking up the Comanche trail was easy enough, but he guessed they'd had a five-hour head start on him. Yet he rode cautiously, scanning every stand of juniper, piñon pine, and every rock formation in the event they had left rear guard sentries to ambush anyone following. But they hadn't, he decided after a few hours and quickened his pace. Because they themselves wouldn't go rescuing any squaw, they probably decided no one else would, Fargo speculated. The day was beginning to wind down as he followed their trail into a long stretch of gamble oak and finally caught sight of them. He slowed, staying plenty far back and saw that they were moving casually. They plainly weren't trying to reach their main camp until the next day. Fargo drew to a halt as he saw the Comanche rein up beside a stream that flowed through the trees.

He swung from the Ovaro, and waited in a thicket of old oaks as the Comanche made camp, letting their ponies loose to graze. He finally spotted Clea in her short nightdress. A Comanche held her by a rawhide thong tied around her neck and as he watched, Fargo saw the Comanche chief pause in front of her, pull the nightgown from her shoulders and fondle her pink, pert breasts. She struck out at him and he laughed as he flung her to the ground, kicking her in the ribs before stalking off. The Comanche holding the rawhide leash pulled her to her feet and led her to a tree a few feet from the stream. Clea tried to pull the nightgown back up over her breasts but the brave stopped her, then tied her hands behind her with another piece of rawhide. He then tied her to the tree with the thong around her neck.

They left her alone, talking among themselves, eating from a leather sack of corn kernels as night fell. Creeping another dozen yards closer, Fargo tethered the Ovaro to a low branch and crawled forward alone. Moonlight filtered through the leaves and gave just enough light for him to see the Comanche spread out their saddle blankets as they lay down to sleep. To the ordinary observer, it would appear that the Comanche had settled themselves down in haphazard fashion but Fargo knew better. The Comanche had arranged themselves in a kind of half wheel around Clea. No one could approach her without coming close to one or another of her captors, too close not to be heard.

Fargo grunted silently in grudging admiration and his eyes dropped to the forest floor. It was thick with dried nut grass. Moving across it in silence would be virtually impossible. He cursed at the Comanche's mastery of trickery and deception. It was what made them different from all other tribes. They could lure their targets to death as no others could. Fargo's lips were pulled back in a grimace as he listened to the camp fall silent. Almost silent, he corrected himself, listening. Only the rushing stream water could be heard.

A tight smile replaced the grimace on his lips. Perhaps their clever trickery could be turned back on them, he muttered inwardly as he continued to listen to the sound that drifted across the carefully positioned sleeping figures. It cloaked the sounds of clacking staghorn beetles and the drone of a hundred kinds of night-flying insects. Fargo listened to the stream for a few more moments as it gurgled and tumbled its way through the trees, then pushed to his feet and backed away from the Comanche. He circled his way to the water, stepping into it and carefully following its path, his steps cloaked by the soft hiss and swish of the water. Only when he was directly behind the tree to which Clea was tied did he step out from the stream. He reached down, drew the thin, double-edged throwing knife from its calf holsters, and slid toward the tree.

Tied in an almost immobile position, Clea didn't hear him as he crept up behind her. He brought his hand around her from behind, and covered her mouth as he whispered in her ear. "Don't make a sound, and don't move," he hissed. He felt her stiffen, and brought the knife up to sever the rawhide thong around her neck, then the others binding her to the tree. He kept hold of her as she turned around, smiling brightly as she pulled the nightgown up in place around herself. Fargo put one finger to his lips. She nodded and followed as he stepped the dozen feet to the stream, and entered the water on his heels. Fargo moved carefully back up the stream until he was far enough from the Comanche before stepping out onto the dry ground. Clea beside him, he was about to start finding his way back to the Ovaro when the sharp cry of alarm shattered the night. It was followed seconds later by more shouts and Fargo cursed silently.

Someone had woken up, or had gone to check on their captive and found her gone. Fargo froze in place, listening, letting his ears tell the story for him as it unfolded. They were all awake now, their initial shouts of alarm dropping down to terse, barely audible exchanges. But his ears told him more. "They're spreading out on foot to find us," he whispered to Clea.

"Why on foot?" she questioned.

"They know we haven't had time to go far, and that we're still on foot. They'd heard our hoofbeats otherwise, and they can do a better job of searching for us on foot," Fargo told her.

"Can we reach your horse?" Clea asked.

"Not likely. They're already coming through the woods. Even if I reached the Ovaro they'd hear us and come chasing. With both of us in the saddle they'd catch up to us quick enough."

"So we just stay here and let them find us?" Clea frowned.

"No. You lay down here and stay flat," he said. "I'll come back for you."

"What are you going to do?" she asked worriedly as she lay herself down on the ground.

"I'm going to try what the army calls diversionary tactics," he said and stepped back into the stream. In a crouch, he moved quickly through the cover of the stream to where the Comanche had been sleeping. Their ponies were loose but huddled together for the night. He drew the Colt as he stepped on tiptoe behind them and fired two shots into the air when he was not more than a foot away. The ponies reared and bolted, and Fargo was back in the stream as the ponies raced off through the woods. He glimpsed the dark forms of running figures racing back through the trees. He had given them two choices—to keep searching for him or go after their ponies.

They did exactly as he had expected, and went running after their ponies, their decision conditioned and instinctual. Recovering their only means of transport was far more important than recapturing a mere white squaw. Fargo hurried upstream again as he listened to the sounds of the Comanche chasing after their mounts, moving away from the campsite. As he reached Clea, she pushed to her feet and came alongside him as he began searching through the dark of the forest for where he had left the Ovaro. "Their ponies won't run all that far," Fargo told her. "But when the Comanche catch up to them, we'll have five or ten minutes on them. That'll be enough for the Ovaro to stay in front carrying the both of us if they decide to come after us." He still caught sounds of the Indians pursuing their ponies through the forest as he searched for the Ovaro. Clea was a few steps behind him as he paused often, using his nose to pick up the horse's scent.

He moved forward, drawing in deep breaths through his nostrils, Clea right at his heels. As his eyes spotted the Ovaro, Fargo's ears suddenly heard the faint hiss of the arrow as it flew through the air. Reacting instantaneously, he flung himself forward in a dive. He felt the pain, sharp and burning, as the arrowhead grazed his temple. Hitting the ground, he rolled, cursing the pain that spread along the side of his head, and came up on one knee to see a Comanche bearing down on him. The man's bow was drawn back to let another arrow fly and Fargo glimpsed the gold amulet against the man's chest. The chief had hung back to wait, and Fargo cursed the man's slyness.

He started to yank the Colt from his holster, but saw he hadn't enough time and rolled again as the arrow tore through the collar of his shirt. He yanked at the Colt again, and once again stopped. Some of the Comanche had caught up to their ponies by now. A shot would tell them exactly where he was and bring them racing back. The time he had bought by sending them chasing their ponies would be nullified. He left the Colt in its holster and flung himself sideways as the Comanche chief's arrow dug deep into the ground inches from his shoulder. As the Comanche used up precious seconds to notch another arrow onto his bowstring, Fargo pulled the thin throwing knife from its calf holster. Using an underhand motion, he sent the knife flying with all his strength.

The Comanche was pulling the bow back to fire again when, out of the corner of his eye, he saw the blade hurtling at him. He tried to turn away but he was too late. The blade hit him in the shoulder, sinking in deep, and the bow dropped from his hands as he fell to one knee. Fargo was on him in one long leap as the Comanche pulled the knife out of his shoulder with a roar of pain and fury. Fargo kicked out, sending the knife flying from the Indian's hand as the Comanche twisted, sprawling facedown on the ground. Fargo scooped up the knife as he ran past the Comanche chief and raced for the Ovaro. Vaulting onto the horse, he saw the Indian still on the ground as Clea ran past him toward the Ovaro. She had almost passed the Indian, whose right shoulder ran thick with blood, when he managed to reach out and close one hand around her ankle.

Clea went down with a cry. The Comanche chief pulled himself forward and was on top of her instantly, his body pressing her facedown on the ground. Astride her, the Indian reached for the tomahawk at his waist. Cursing, Fargo pulled the big Henry from its saddle case, even as he knew he still didn't want the sound of a shot warning others where they were. The chief had the tomahawk in his right hand when he discovered he couldn't bring his arm up high enough to use his weapon because of his injured shoulder. He needed to transfer the weapon to his left hand so he could raise it high enough to crash it down on Clea's skull.

But the extra time had given Fargo the few seconds he needed. Holding the rifle as though it were an awkwardly shaped lance, he sent it hurtling through the air, the long barrel first. The Comanche, his left arm raised, was about to bring the short-handled ax down on Clea's head when the barrel of the heavy rifle slammed into the side of his face, splitting his cheekbone. Blood erupted from his face and he toppled sideways, away from Clea, the rifle falling to the ground. Clea was pushing to her feet when Fargo reached her. He scooped up the rifle as he pulled her into the saddle with him. Racing the pinto forward, he glanced back to see the Comanche chief on all fours, shaking his head as blood streamed from his shoulder and the side of his face.

Fargo was confident the chief wouldn't be giving immediate chase until his men arrived with their mounts, and he slowed the pinto down to a steady canter. Clea was silent as they rode until, when dawn streaked the sky, Fargo halted and used his canteen to let the Ovaro drink. "I'm sorry," Fargo heard her say, her voice small and contrite.

"You should be," he muttered. "Thought you had more sense."

"I wanted everything ready to get an early start," she said. "Thanks for coming after me." She kissed him, clinging to his lips before finally drawing back. "It wasn't easy, I'll bet," Clea said.

"Let's just say it wasn't a unanimous decision," he answered wryly.

"But you came. I'll make that up to you," Clea said.

"Not for a while. We've a lot of ground to cover before all of this is over," he said. "You're here. That's what counts. The Comanche lost out again. We just got lucky," Fargo continued, moving the pinto forward.

"Maybe there is something to Solita's fetish," Clea murmured soberly. She fell silent as the pinto held the pace until the sun grew burning hot overhead. Fargo had the horse back to a walk when they reached the wagons. As Clea slid from the saddle, Harry Paxton was the first to reach her, embracing her in a bear hug as a small cheer rose from the others. The wagons still in place, Fargo rode to the rock wall and dismounted and unsaddled the Ovaro as Solita came up to him.

"I was going to go on if you hadn't arrived within another hour," she said, her face beautifully expressionless.

"Now you don't have to wait," he said. "Stay northeast. I'll catch up."

Solita's frown was instant. "What are you going to do?"

"Get me some sleep," he said. "It wasn't exactly a cakewalk."

"I'm sure," she said, pausing a moment. "I haven't changed my opinion about anything, you know," she said.

"Didn't expect you would," Fargo replied.

"You had no right to go after her. Your obligation

was to me and the agreement you made. I can't trust in you the way I did before," Solita said reproachfully.

"I might earn it back. You never know—I might do something right," he said evenly and she acknowledged the barb with a moment's tightening of her finely etched lips. But she walked away with her face set and he watched the slender beauty of her body that seemed to sway to its own inner music. Soon after, she led the wagons away, and Fargo saw that some of the wounded still rode inside the wagons. When they were out of sight, he found a spot hidden away among the rocks where he could safely sleep, yet where any sound below would echo up to him.

No sounds awoke him and the sun was in the afternoon sky when he rose and scanned the hills below. Nothing moved. The Comanche hadn't returned to try a quick pursuit again. A small victory, he knew, as he saddled the Ovaro and began to ride out of the Red Hills. There was still daylight left when he caught up to the wagons and saw the questions in Solita's ebony eyes. "No sign of them," he said.

"They've given up," she said.

"Maybe. For now, anyway," he said.

"You're a hard man to satisfy." She sniffed.

"When it comes to the Comanche, I don't take any chances."

"You really think they'll come back to try again?" she asked.

"You never are sure with the Comanche," he said and pointed to a large stand of burr oak. "Make camp there," he directed and Benton took the wagons into the trees as the day began to fade. Fargo bedded down off by himself and before the cook fires were lit, Solita appeared with her map of scraggly lines.

"Here," she said, pointing to a spot on the primitive map. "Wichita. The conquistadores that returned made better maps." Fargo studied the scrawled, erratic markings on her map until darkness came.

"That spot is past Wichita," he said and she frowned back, folding the piece of parchment. "You're lucky it isn't in Wichita."

"Why?" she questioned sharply.

"Wichita's a built-up cow town. You'd never find a damn thing there even if they let you dig up the place, which they wouldn't," Fargo answered. "I've seen maps such as yours before. Indians drew them. Some of the early French trappers, too. They all made the same marks for the same things . . . mountains. In this case, it'd be the Flint Hills. They're past Wichita. It'd be the logical place for them to stop for a last stand. That's what it was, wasn't it?"

"No one's sure. We know it's where Coronado turned back empty-handed. We don't know anything more," Solita said.

"Did Coronado catch the Aztecs there?" Fargo questioned.

Solita's face tightened. "Neither conquistador writings nor Aztec reports make that clear, but it's what I'm going to find out," she said with sudden vehemence. "As part of the historical study," she added, almost as a hasty afterthought, Fargo noted as she hurried away, carrying her ancient map. He wandered to the chuck wagon for a plate and supper, and received another stolen kiss from Clea behind the wagon.

"Saw her talking to you. She give you trouble for coming after me?" Clea asked.

"Not this time. She was showing me a map," he said.

"Learn anything interesting?" Clea asked.

"Not a lot," he said as the others in line sent him moving on with his plate. Fargo bedded down soon after the meal ended, and slept soundly, feeling refreshed when he took to the saddle in the morning. He led the way, riding out in front of the wagons, leaving them out of sight behind him as he surveyed the terrain. He found mostly flat ground bordered by increasingly heavy stands of hackberry and ironwood. The day slid into late afternoon and Fargo was just allowing himself to feel optimistic when it happened. A dark, dank odor filled the air, the smell of charred wood and soil made acrid with layers of ash.

It hung like an invisible curtain through which Fargo had to pass and when he pulled to a halt he felt a sickening feeling in the pit of his stomach. He stared at what had once been a vast forest, but was now only an endless expanse of blackened stumps that stretched as far as the eye could see. Here and there, the trunk of a branchless tree rose up, a pathetic reminder of what it had once been. Besides the acres upon acres of burnt stumps, he became aware of the eerie silence that had descended upon the land. Nothing moved in the terrible graveyard that had once teemed with life. Not a single shrew, fox, deer, or mole stirred. Not a single bird flew over branches that had once been a nesting home. Not a single insect buzzed, droned, or clicked. The silence of nature's tomb was deafening.

Fargo surveyed the bleak scene and knew that lightning had probably started the forest blaze. It had happened sometime within the month, he guessed, drawing in the character of the odor. He was surveying the grim scene when Solita arrived with the wagons and stared in horror. "My God," she breathed.

"We'll have to go around it," Fargo said.

"That'd take us out of our way," Solita said.

"That's right." He nodded.

"How far out of our way? How long would it take?" she pressed.

He shrugged. "Can't say. I can't see the end of it. Days, at least, maybe a week before we work our way back."

"No, I'm not taking days off our schedule. Absolutely not. We'll go through," Solita said.

"You can't. You'll be going over nothing but stumps. Your wagons will never take it. Their axles will break. You can't even bed down in all that ash," Fargo said.

"We can and we will," she snapped.

"You won't be able to breathe, even if you find a place to bed down," he told her.

"We'll sleep in the wagons, taking turns if we have to," she said. "I'm not losing days, maybe a week, not now when I'm getting close. The day's almost over. We'll camp here and go through in the morning."

She turned to bark orders at Benton and he had the wagons roll up to the hackberry stand, still thick and green and untouched by the fire. Fargo dismounted, pausing beside her. "What happens when your wagons break down?" he asked.

"They won't. You're being overly cautious, Fargo," Solita said before simply walking away. Fargo saw Clea positioning the chuck wagon against the trees and strolled over to her as the dusk began to fade into twilight.

"Seems you've been overruled," Clea said with a touch of rakishness.

"That doesn't bother me. I hope to hell she's right," Fargo said.

"But you don't think so."

"I sure don't. Something's driving her. She's almost obsessed and I don't understand it. I'd feel a lot better if I knew what that is," Fargo said.

"Maybe those saddlebags of hers hold the answer. You ought to go through them," Clea said.

"No chance of that. She guards them carefully, practically sleeps with them," Fargo said.

"Maybe there's a way," Clea said almost casually and he frowned back and waited for her to go on. "Put her into the kind of deep sleep where she won't hear you," Clea finished.

"You mean drug her?" Fargo frowned.

Clea shrugged. "How badly do you want to know what's driving her?" she pushed at him.

Fargo thought for a moment and realized he was feeling both ashamed and intrigued, and decided to fall back on being honest and glib. "Badly enough, but I don't go around carrying drugs on me," he said.

"I can help you," Clea said, refusing to let him drop the subject. "We carry a supply of things in the wagon for emergencies, sickness, if somebody's cut, can't sleep, had stomach spasms, whatever. I've monkshood and opium."

"You're serious, aren't you?" Fargo said.

"I thought you'd be, too," Clea returned. "I can put some opium in her coffee and she's knocked out till morning."

Fargo frowned into the night, aware his thoughts were racing but only in one direction. Finding out what was driving Solita was growing increasingly important. Not just for him, but for the good of the whole crew. Knowing might well answer all those strange coincidences that had been at the heart of everything that had occurred. As time went on, Solita had become more and more driven, increasingly uncaring about anyone or anything except her goal. She had been willing to sacrifice Clea to the Comanche for it. And for what? Fargo asked himself once again. A field expedition that was essentially scholarly in nature? It didn't fit then and it fit even less now.

Now she was again ready to put everyone through unnecessary danger and hardship. Why? The question grew larger as Fargo considered it. He had an obligation to try and find an answer before her unexplainable obsession brought new and equally ruthless excesses. His thoughts broke off and he peered at Clea, seeing her watching him with something close to amused speculation in her eyes. "Do it," he said and she nodded. "You were hoping I'd say that," he added and her little smile was an admission. "Why?" he pressed.

"Because you deserve to know," she said.

He reached out and caught her wrist. "This is strictly between us. That includes Harry," he said.

"Absolutely," she said, then pulled away and hurried to the rear of the wagon where Benton's men were lining up to be served. Fargo bedded down by himself, away from everyone else, waiting until the last man had been served before he returned to the chuck wagon. Clea saw him approach, and went behind the horses where they had been unhitched. She handed him a small object wrapped in cloth. "It's done. Wait an hour for it to kick in," she murmured and he hurried away. Returning to his bedroll, he found the package to be a small, square candle. He lay back, dozed, and let a little more than an hour pass before he rose and crept along the line of wagons.

Searching under a half-moon, he found Solita beneath a blanket set back in the trees. He dropped down to one knee beside her, and watched her even breathing. In repose, her face was strikingly beautiful, her shoulders bare and beautifully sculpted. The two saddlebags lay tight against her as she slept. He started to reach out when he saw the derringer nestled in her right hand and he blanched, praying that Clea's potion had taken effect. If it hadn't, Solita would snap awake, shooting in an automatic reaction to an intruder. Ever so gingerly, he started to slide the first saddlebag out from under her arm. She didn't stir, he saw with relief, and he used one hand to cradle her head as he pulled the second bag free.

He walked away a dozen yards before he halted, lighted the candle, and began to rifle through the saddlebags. He knew he'd be searching for any answers to the questions that had bothered him at the outset—the vagueness in her replies, the name of the university that had given her the grant for the project, all the coincidences that bothered him then continued to bother him now, and lastly, the reason to what was driving her. The flickering light first revealed to him withered pages of faded writing, all in Spanish, all plainly reports from the conquistadores. Next, he found even older pages of crumbling parchment. These were covered with Aztec glyphs that were meaningless to him. The second bag held Solita's mountain lion fetish, all the ancient maps, two sheets of what seemed like some sort of list, and a half-dozen strings of beads and amulets.

He was about to close the bag when his fingers touched upon an envelope that was neither crumbling nor deteriorating. He opened it, and pulled out a sheet of paper written in clear, fresh ink. He felt a stab of excitement as he thought he had found the communication from the university, but he quickly realized he hadn't. His frown deepened as he read:

Solita Chiltec,
    Here is the bank draft. This will finance all your costs for the project. As we agreed, I get fifty

percent of everything. I'm counting on your esti-
mates. They better be right.

I don't put out good money without results. I
don't get cheated, either. Remember that.

Santos Arriaga

Fargo reread the letter before he put it back in the
envelope and returned it to the saddlebags. It gave
one answer. No university had given her a grant for
the project. A man named Santos Arriaga had fi-
nanced her and from the tone of the agreement, Arriaga was a man of suspicion and threats. Fargo
returned to where Solita was still fast asleep, carefully
placing the bags back with her, and hurried away.

He had found precious little, he realized, except for
one thing: Solita's project was a facade. All the scientific collecting of information on plants, trees, birds,
and animals was just going through motions, all designed to keep up the pretense. That fact only opened
up a new bushel of questions. If she didn't give a
damn about following the path of the conquistadores
as they pursued the Aztecs, then what was she doing?
Why this elaborate deception? Was it really a deception? Her attention to everything they found and to
every place they stopped was certainly real. Her in-
volvement in tracking the trail of the conquistadores
was too intense to be an act. Yet he knew now that no
university waited for the scientific details she'd col-
lected. What did it all mean? Fargo pondered, cursing
at having yet more questions that needed answers.

But one thing had crystallized inside him. He had

come this far. He'd see it through. Besides, he'd been paid to do that and he'd hold to his part of the bargain. Only now he had more reason to do so. He returned to his bedroll to find Clea's tight little form waiting for him. "Didn't expect you," he said, his surprise honest.

"I'm curious. That's always been a part of me. What did you find out?" she asked.

"Not much, I'm afraid," Fargo answered. "You ever hear the name Santos Arriaga?"

"Why would I?" Clea said quickly, defensiveness instantly edging her voice. He threw her a sharp glance. It was the same kind of instant defensiveness he got from her when he'd wondered why there were so many attempts at halting a scholarly expedition. *I wouldn't know about that*, she had snapped, though he hadn't implied she would. Suddenly he found himself wondering about a lot of things. Was her waiting here for him really just idle curiosity? She was the one who had volunteered giving the potion to keep Solita asleep, after all. Had it been just as a favor to him? Or a way to find out things for herself? Maybe there were more tangled threads than he'd suspected on this journey.

Clea's voice broke into his thoughts. "Who is this Santos Arriaga?" she asked and Fargo almost smiled at how quickly she'd switched from defensiveness to exaggerated casualness.

"He wrote Solita a letter," Fargo said. "Didn't say anything much, nothing about himself. Thought you might've heard the name somewhere."

"Sorry," she said as she came to him, her arms encircling his neck, her firm, round breasts laying softly against his chest. "No sense wasting opportunities."

"She was starting to wake when I left," Fargo lied and Clea drew back.

"I'm surprised." She frowned.

"Everyone reacts to opium differently," he remarked.

She thought over his answer before nodding. "True enough," she said, then kissed him and hurried on, her tight little figure bouncing away. Fargo drew a deep breath through tight lips. He'd keep what he'd learned to himself, he decided, at least until he knew more. Clea had suddenly become a puzzle herself, one he had to solve before he could trust her. The development left a bitter taste in his mouth, and a residue of disappointment. Perhaps he was being too harsh, he admitted, but he didn't need more question marks to deal with.

But if Clea had become a puzzle, Solita had become a full-blown enigma. There was no question which he'd try to solve first.

12

Solita appeared rested when Fargo halted before her in the morning. Sleeping potions had their positive effects as well, he noted silently. He saw her studying his face as he surveyed the acres of blackened land, and his face hardened as he brought his gaze back to her.

"You're making a bad mistake," he said.

"It's my decision to make," she said.

"You hired me for what I know, remember?"

"But not to make decisions for me," she said haughtily. "Of course, I'd like you to believe in me."

"I'd like you to listen to me," he replied. Her fine-lined lips pressed together as she turned away. Fargo strode over to the chuck wagon where Harry Paxton handed him a tin mug of coffee. Clea waved as she finished washing breakfast mugs. "Wrap as many of your pots and kettles as you can. Take extra kerchiefs for yourselves," he said and hurried away before they could question him about his directions. He used his canteen to let the Ovaro drink, then swung into the saddle and rode to where Solita was giving Matt Benton the signal to go forward.

He let her stay in the lead and moved back and forth along the line of wagons and riders. Most of the wounded had been able to return to their horses, but a few still rode inside the wagons. Fargo watched as the procession started into the vast expanse of charred land and he spurred the pinto forward, his eyes scanning the ground. He saw prints where a few riders had entered but quickly turned back, and he grimaced as his eyes swept the gray ashes coating over every inch of the soil. Falling back, Fargo watched as the wagons began to roll over stump after stump. "Slow, go slow!" he shouted but he knew the advice was hollow. No matter how slowly they moved, wagons would come down hard after climbing over each stump, and he heard wheels creak, axles grind and wagon frames shudder.

But there was no other way around the punishing stumps that covered the forest floor. They hadn't moved far into the blackened forest when the thing Fargo had been most afraid of began to occur and he cursed at the sight of it. Slowly, like a fog gathering itself, the deep pall of ashes that covered the ground began to rise into the air. Stirred and disturbed by wagon wheels and hooves, the carpet of fine ash loosed itself into thick clouds. But this was no fog. This was a deadly spectre that choked, clung, enveloped, and overwhelmed eyes, noses, and mouths, clogging pores, and coating everything it touched in gray. It ascended in silence, turning the world gray in a matter of minutes.

Fargo tied his kerchief over his face, and saw others

hurrying to do the same. A few of Benton's men turned their coat collars up. It wouldn't be enough, Fargo muttered. It was only a few minutes more when he heard the horses blowing and snorting hard as they fought to breathe. He could only see the wagons as murky shapes in the gray world of ash that rose with new thickness the more it was disturbed. Moving in closer, Fargo saw that Solita was still in the lead. She had wrapped her entire head in a silk scarf that let her see through its fine weave. He saw her shaking her head as the material let ash sift through it.

He peered at one of the wagons, and saw that the diggers inside it had laid facedown. But there was no escaping the choking ash that permeated everything. It was a world of strange, eerie silence broken only by the snorting of the horses and the heavy thump of the wagons as they clambered over stumps. Fargo was not far from one wagon when he heard a splintering sound, and he turned to see it list to one side as the rear wheel snapped in two. The driver halted and Fargo saw that there were three more men in the wagon as Solita rode up. "Forget about fixing it," Fargo told her, his voice muffled behind the kerchief.

"Any ideas?" Solita asked.

"Everybody stays where they are. You stop stirring up the ash and it'll settle down in a few hours. Then we go back before there are more breakdowns," Fargo said.

"Absolutely not," Solita said, her voice sharp even under the scarf. "Unhitch the horses. The men can ride them, two to a horse."

"You've a lot of your artifacts in the wagon," Fargo said.

"They can stay here for now. We'll come back for them," she said. He grunted angrily at the glibness of her answer. "Get the horses unhitched," Solita barked at the driver and backed away. Fargo watched the gray figures loosen harnesses and climb onto the horses, moving on as Solita beckoned everyone forward. The abandoned wagon seemed like a symbol to Fargo as he moved on, echoing Solita's abandonment of her pretensions that this was solely a scientific exploration. He wondered how long the others could hold out.

He had only five minutes to have the question answered as another of the wagons broke down, this one with the rear axle splitting as it hit a high stump. Both wheels flew off and the rims and felloes broke away. Solita rode back to inspect the wagon, now impaled upon the high stump, and her solution was the same. The horses were unhitched and those inside the wagons rode. As they went on, Fargo realized that turning back was no longer a choice. They had come too far and he peered ahead, straining his eyes, but the ash curtain refused to be pierced.

He rode on slowly for perhaps another hundred yards when he heard a heavy thump from behind him, followed almost instantly by another. He shouted through his handkerchief before he turned to look behind him, certain what the sound meant. When he wheeled the Ovaro around he saw two men on the ash-covered ground where they had dropped from their horses. Dismounting, he knelt beside the first man, and bent forward to listen, hoping for the sound of choking, gasping breath. But there was none and he saw that the man had been using only his turned-up coat collar to shield his mouth. Too much ash had filtered into his throat and lungs, snuffing out his ability to breathe, just as a candle is snuffed out.

The second prone figure was the same, Fargo saw, and he rose as Solita rode up. He climbed onto the Ovaro, faced her, and let his silence speak for him. She turned away and he followed her to the head of the column. "We can't stop now," she said.

"Can't or won't?" he said.

"Both," she spat. Fargo seethed silently. She had to know her wrongheaded decisions had brought them to this. She had to know she should have listened to him. But whatever drove her also refused to allow that admission.

"You can't just go on taking in more of this ash," he told her. "Your people will be dropping like flies. None of Benton's men are youngsters. I'll bet most have their health already ruined by smoking, chewing tobacco, and too much rot-gut whiskey. They'll never be able to take much more. None of us will."

Solita said nothing but her eyes stayed on him in a kind of unwilling plea. Maybe there was no answer, no way out, Fargo pondered. He couldn't see clearly behind the silk scarf that wrapped around her face but if he could, he wagered he'd see a realization that they could be looking into the gray, ashen face of death. It would be a grudging realization, he was certain. But his own thoughts grew dark. He had no ready solutions, perhaps none at all. Only one avenue held any hope but he had to know one thing, first. That meant finding out if distance and time gave them a chance to survive. As his plans took shape, he turned to Solita again.

"Everybody stays here," he said.

"Where are you going?" she asked quickly.

"To find out if we have a chance. I'll come back and tell you, either way," he said grimly. "Meanwhile, stay in place, don't move around, and breathe as little as you can."

He walked the Ovaro forward, keeping the horse at a slow, step-by-step pace. One horse moving slowly wouldn't stir up the deadly cloud of ash, and after a few minutes he cut through the gray curtain to see the land ahead. Only more acres of blackened and burnt land greeted him, but at least he could see where he was going. He was glad to see the sun was still in the sky as he plodded on, the pinto's hooves sending up little spirals of ash with every step. But he felt the horse's chest expand as the Ovaro gratefully drew in relatively clean air, even though the odor of burnt wood still lingered heavily.

Fargo kept moving in as straight a line as the decimated stumps would permit, easing his way through the charred forest that seemed it would never end. He was about to halt and turn back in defeat when he glimpsed an opening where the burnt land came to an end. Green grass and full, thick burr oaks rose up beyond, and he hurried forward to halt at the edge of the free-ravaged forest. He stared at the verdant, lush land like a starving man looks at a piece of grilled, sizzling beef. Gazing beyond the first expanse of grass, he saw sunlight along a distant river, probably an extension of the Salt Fork, he guessed.

Fargo turned the pinto and looked back the way he had come, trying to estimate how far he had ridden. Everything depended on the distance, he realized with a bitter taste in his mouth. The difference between life and death would be a matter of how far it was to the untouched forests. The wagons were too far away to inch their way. The choking, insidiously suffocating ash would take its fatal toll before they were halfway out of the burnt forest. They had but one chance—to race hell-bent for where he stood. But it would truly be a race against death. Was it a race they could win? Fargo had to ask himself. Was survival too far away for them? Could flesh and blood, both two-legged and four-legged, defy distance and nature's power?

The questions revolved in Fargo's mind as he realized he had only one choice: He had to lead them in the most desperate race of their lives. They could either die one by one on their slow march or try to outrun death. It was a devil's choice, he realized, but they had no other. He cast a last glance at the sun, and estimated that it would be at the horizon when and if they made it back. Drawing deep breaths of fresh air into his lungs, Fargo began the slow, careful ride back into the scarred and seared forest. Trying to disturb the ash as little as possible, he forced himself to keep the pinto at a walk. Time seemed to stand still, and he cursed as he saw how little he had traveled. The spectre of distance haunted him as he rode, his hands stiff on the reins, as the world turned gray again, the curtain of ash still hanging in the air ahead of him.

Moving into the heavy clouds of ash-filled air, Fargo finally discerned the gray shapes of the wagons, then the horsemen nearby. No one moved but he felt their eyes boring into him. Finally Solita pushed her mount forward. "Another of Matt's men dropped," she murmured.

"Only one?" he asked and hated himself for the callous bitterness of the question. He let his eyes flick to the others as he spoke to Solita. "Here's the picture. It's not a good one. You'll never make it going ahead slowly. You'll all die one by one. This damn ash will get to you—to all of us—before we get out of here. But there's one chance—to make a run for it. It won't be an ordinary run. You'll have to ride like you've never ridden before. Either you'll make it in time or you won't. It's a good ways on."

"You going to take us?" someone called.

"I'll try, but you'll really be on your own," Fargo said. "Here's what you're going to do. You ride all out. Don't stop for anything or anybody. The wheels come off your wagons, you keep going. Your wagons break in half, you keep going. Your horse drops, you jump off and keep running. You'll be stirring up every damn piece of ash there is, but this is the only chance. If it isn't too far away, and we can ride fast enough, we'll make it. Otherwise, we'll be meeting in that last

218

roundup in the sky that the preachers keep talking about."

He fell silent, letting his words sink in while the one question continued to reverberate in his thoughts. *Was* it too far? Were they doomed before they started? He wasn't at all sure that even the Ovaro's powerful lungs could withstand the furious dash through the suffocating, choking ash. He wheeled the pinto in a tight circle and Solita paused beside him. "Thanks for everything," she said.

"I'm thinking it's not time for thanks, not yet. It's too early," he said.

"No it's not, no matter how it ends," she said, a simple sincerity in her voice he'd never heard before. He moved out in front of the others.

"On three, give it everything you've got," he said, pulling the kerchief tight around his face. Then he lifted his voice. "One, two, *three.*" With the last word, he put the Ovaro into an instant gallop, letting the horse go at its will, skirting some stumps, jumping others, running right over still others. Glancing back as much as he did forward, he saw that Matt Benton and his men were racing their already labored horses. The animals chests heaved as they sought to draw in enough clear air to breathe. Fargo looked over at the wagons that bounced and shook and creaked and groaned as they careened over the forest floor at full speed.

At every fallen tree and stump, their frame bodies swerved and bounced high into the air, sending ash whirling into the air in a frenzy of blanketing, suffocating gray. Fargo tried to breathe inside his kerchief as much as he could to avoid drawing in more of the ash, and he cursed as he felt the Ovaro start to shorten its stride. He looked back to see two of Benton's men go down as their horses dropped. The men pushed to their feet but only managed to run a few yards before they, too, collapsed and lay still. He had barely turned his attention back to the Ovaro when splintered sounds pierced the murky haze, and he looked back to see the two wagons crash almost simultaneously, both shattering into pieces as they came down hard on high stumps.

The two drivers held on to their horses as they straddled the two front wheels, the only remains of their wagons. As he watched, the wheels spun off their axles and both drivers pitched to the ground. They struggled to rise but managed only to crawl until they stopped, too. He caught sight of another wagon as it went over on its side and broke into pieces, the driver disappearing underneath it. The ash had become so thick Fargo could barely see through it, but his ears told him three more horses collapsed and he glimpsed two figures staggering forward on foot. The sound of another wagon smashing to pieces came to him as he bent forward in the saddle, concern sweeping over him as he listened to the Ovaro's increasingly harsh breathing.

Fargo grimaced as he kept the horse barrelling forward. It was not a matter of choice any longer. It was the only way left. Caring, compassion, mercy, sympathy—those things no longer counted. Only the headlong race for survival existed. Shutting his ears to the sounds of failure echoing behind him, Fargo kept the Ovaro moving, unaware of how much time had passed, when he finally saw the gray curtain come to an end. Dim light pierced it, first, then as it shredded, he saw the green forest ahead and soon he was bursting into the clear, clean open. His lungs eagerly filled with fresh air and the pain in his chest immediately lessened. He slowed the Ovaro and felt the horse's ribs expand.

But the ash still lay upon and inside both horse and rider as Fargo moved forward through the last of the daylight toward the distant river, green burr oak and ironwood framing its banks. Looking back, he saw a handful of figures lurch into the open air, including Matt Benton and a few of his men, all stumbling as they walked. Fargo's eyes swept the open land past the end of the burned forest and found Solita just as she emerged into the clear a dozen yards below where he'd halted. She was hunched low over her saddle but she still held the reins of the packhorse, he noted. A few more figures emerged on foot, then another on horseback. His eyes widened in astonishment as he saw the chuck wagon appear in one piece, the two gray-shrouded figures atop the buckboard huddled side by side, wrapped together in a blanket.

Pulling the kerchief from his face, Fargo called out, his voice a dry, cracked squeak, and he pointed to the river still visible in the fast-fading dusk. There was no need to tell them what to do and they followed as he pointed the Ovaro toward the water. Night descended quickly as he reached the river and Fargo rode the horse into the water, slid from the saddle with all his clothes on and gave a groan of relief as the water washed the clinging ash from him. Shedding his clothes in the water, then throwing them onto the riverbank, he could faintly make out the figures in the darkness that were now also plunging fully clothed into the river. Fargo swam, letting the river sweep every speck of ash from his body, and he saw the Ovaro not far away shake and roll in the welcome freshness of the water.

Finally finished, he climbed onto the shore, and called the Ovaro over to him. He reached into his saddlebag and pulled out a blanket that had stayed dry at the bottom of the bag, and wrapped himself in it as he lay down on the mossy riverbank. Other crew members finally emerged from the water, the moon too shrouded by clouds to see anyone clearly as they began spreading clothes on the moss to dry. The first two that came to him were Harry Paxton and Clea, both now wrapped in individual blankets. They stopped before him, and in Harry Paxton's drawn face Fargo saw memories and horror that would never completely go away. Even Clea's usual tomboy flair had left her, leaving a haunted soberness in her youthful face.

"How'd you do it? You were in the heaviest, most cumbersome of all the wagons, the one I never figured would make it," Fargo asked.

"Plain dumb luck or the Good Lord riding with us," Harry Paxton replied. His eyes moved across the riverbank. "The wagon came through but there's hardly anybody left to cook for," he observed grimly.

"Sleep late. Let the sun dry out your things," Fargo said.

"What happens now?" Clea queried.

"What do you think?" Fargo said sharply. "She'll want to go on, especially after we came through this."

"Why not?" Clea shrugged and Fargo felt surprise push into him. He'd expected bitter disagreement, certainly angry resentment, but Clea's shrug had been acceptance if not almost sympathy. He lay back as Clea and Harry walked away, still wrestling with his surprise when he heard soft footsteps nearing him. He sat up to see Solita. Even wrapped tightly in a blanket, she looked regal, and in control, he marveled.

"We saved a week," she said. "That's important."

"Pretty damn high price to pay, I'd say," he returned.

"I know what you're thinking," she said almost disapprovingly.

"Tell me. I'm not sure myself," he snapped.

"It was all my fault for not listening to you," she said coolly.

"That's pretty much it. You saying that's wrong?" he asked.

"I'm saying it had to be," she answered.

"The dead would probably disagree," he snapped.

She didn't flinch, not letting either remorse or concession disturb the composed beauty of her face. "It doesn't change anything. We go on come morning," she said.

"I expected that," he said.

"Good," Solita said, and started to turn away but

223

halted. "We do what we have to do. That can be its own burden. Sometimes others suffer for it," she said.

"That some kind of excuse?" he said harshly.

"No, no excuse. Just a fact," she said. Fargo watched her disappear in the darkness, then heard a noise and saw an empty wagon and its team slowly appear, somehow emerging from the burned forest on their own. He watched the horses go to the river and drink, then finally wander off to stand quietly. Finding a spot under a wide-branched ironwood near where he'd put his clothes, Fargo lay down on his bedroll and embraced sleep.

He slept into the morning sun, and his clothes were dry when he woke. Harry Paxton had coffee ready and as Fargo sipped from the tin cup he surveyed the scene. He counted Matt Benton, three of his men, one of the diggers, Harry and Clea, and the one, lone wagon that had appeared and the chuck wagon. He was taking in the grim scene as Solita came up to him. "Not much left," he commented and his eyes noted the slow movements of the men, their faces drawn and haunted. They were men who had stared death in the face and would never be the same for it. Fargo turned to Solita. "Let them go their way. I'll go on with you," he said.

"Of course you will. You made an agreement and I need you. But they go along, too. I'll need help bringing things back," she said sharply. Fargo made a derisive sound. She was sticking to her facade. Fargo was still wondering at her motives when Clea surprised him again.

"We'll go along. We've come this far. We'd like to see the finish," she said.

"That's settled," Solita said and tossed him a glance that held smug triumph, and something more he couldn't define. She stalked off to get her horses and Fargo focused a probing glance at Clea. She was rapidly growing harder to understand as well, and he felt a definite uneasiness about her, now. But he'd still concentrate on unraveling Solita, he reminded himself as he saddled the Ovaro. He was ready when Solita waved the others forward.

Two of Matt Benton's men rode inside the lone wagon that had appeared, and Clea and Harry took up the rear in the chuck wagon. Fargo rode past the scraggly little procession and led the way into flat, easy-riding terrain. Rich forests and long stretches of rock formations dotted the land as he rode on ahead of the others. He led the way around Wichita and toward Flint Hills, terrain that was perfect for making good time. But, with the ingrained habits of the Trailsman, Fargo's eyes scoured the land, taking note of deer tracks, the prints of raccoons and badgers, and the occasional mark of a black bear.

But he felt a furrow crease his brow as he saw something more in the land, not fashioned of tracks or prints, yet its own kind of trail. It was a trail that sent a shiver through him and he immediately hoped he was seeing more than there was. Fargo halted, swung from the saddle, and peered at the ground, his eyes following the unusual number of fissures that crossed the topsoil. Kneeling down, he ran his fingers along

225

the lines, most of them still very thin threads. They were all new, none more than a few weeks old, he saw. He followed the fissures, halting again where a new set crossed the first ones. This time he saw thin wisps of steam rising up from a couple of the cracks.

He passed his hands over the spirals of steam and felt the heat in them. Pressing his palms on the soil, he found that it, too, was warm. But not the warmth of good, rich topsoil. This was a warmth that filtrated up from far below the earth's crust. Fargo gave a deep frown. He had seen this network of fissures before. They always meant one thing and he rose as he saw Solita and the others come into view. He waved them forward and turned to ride on ahead again. As he rode, his eyes sweeping the ground, he saw the veined lines almost disappear only to appear again an hour later. This time, the fissures were deeper and wider, and steam rose from a dozen of them. He dismounted again, pressed his hands to the topsoil and felt the heat of it, and his lips pulled back in a grimace as he rode on.

The day was drawing to a close. Fargo was kneeling, hands pressed to the ground, as Solita rode up. "What are you doing?" she frowned.

"Feeling for vibrations," he said.

"Vibrations?" she echoed.

"The kind that mean an earthquake. I've been seeing all the other signs," he said and saw a shadow of alarm come into Solita's face.

"Maybe they don't mean what you think they do," she said.

"I'll need more signs to be sure," he said.

"What if you find more?"

"I'll say we get the hell out of this whole area."

"Ridiculous. Signs are signs. They might mean nothing for months," she scoffed.

"These are too active," Fargo said.

"How long before we reach Flint Hills?" she asked.

"By tomorrow night," he told her.

"Then we double the pace tomorrow," she said, motioning for the others to make camp as night fell. Harry prepared a small meal. No one's appetite had really returned, and Fargo distanced himself from the others as he bedded down. He slept, setting his inner alarm clock to wake him when the moon passed the midnight sky. He rose right on time, silently moving away from the others sleeping nearby. When he was far enough away, he slowly began to examine the ground again, sometimes moving on hands and knees. He felt, pressed, poked, and turned over topsoil, watching the steam spiral from fissures. He had a very definite purpose—to examine the land when the sun no longer burned down on it.

The burning rays of the sun penetrated the earth deeply, bringing nourishment to the soil and everything that lived on it and in it. But it could also mislead, its warming blanket deceiving. He had to know the reality of the situation now, when the sun had been gone for six hours, giving the ground plenty of time to cool under the pale moon. He continued to probe and when he finished, his worries had not abated. The sun wasn't the reason for the warmth he had found in the soil. It was almost as warm as it had been when he probed during the sun-drenched day. His fears had been confirmed. This was a warmth rising from deep below the earth's surface, a heat generated by the friction of vast subterranean tectonic plates moving against each other.

Their movement against each other, pulverizing rocks and soil as they did, eventually sent the earth above into the disastrous upheaval called earthquakes. Fargo rose and returned to his bedroll. He had determined enough to make him both satisfied and unhappy. Earthquake activity was certainly taking place. When it would erupt remained an unanswerable question, so he forced himself to sleep, knowing he could bring no answers. When morning came, Fargo sought out Solita and she tossed the question at him. "When?" she demanded.

"Tomorrow. Months from tomorrow. Or it could subside without bringing a quake," he answered honestly.

"Which means you really don't know anything," she snapped.

"I know I don't favor waiting around to find out," he said.

"I'll take my chances," she said. "Let's make up some time." She left him and hurried on, and he fell in with the others as they followed her. He brought the pinto alongside the chuck wagon, where Clea sat on the tailgate.

"What makes you so anxious to be in on the finish?" he asked her. "I'd have thought you'd jump at the chance to get away from Solita as soon as you could."

"I told you, I'm just naturally curious," she answered offhandedly.

"What if I said I was going to cut out? Would you go with me?" he slid at her.

Her glance was sharp, a crease touching her brow. He waited, hoping her answer might reveal something. It had put her on more of a spot than she realized. "I'm not answering that," she said. "You're not about to cut out on her. That wouldn't be like you. Give me something you mean and I'll answer you."

He swore silently, and managed a smile. She was being very clever or coyly female. Or both. He'd not find that out, he knew, and sent the pinto forward to ride just abreast of Solita. She held the brisk pace she'd said she was going to keep, but the afternoon was growing long before they neared Flint Hills. Fargo had spent a good part of the day scanning the ground with increasingly unhappy results. When he spotted a particularly large fissure sending up a wide column of hot steam, he drew to a halt. She saw him inspecting it, and reined up. "I'm going on," she said, annoyance in her voice.

"I'll catch up." He nodded and dismounted. The others followed as she rode on. Fargo first knelt on the ground, then stretched out beside the fissure, staying as close to the steam as he could without getting scalded. His ear against the ground, he lay for some twenty minutes before he felt rather than heard the sound—a sudden series of vibrations that trembled through the earth. They lasted a few minutes, coming and going and then finally halting. They were not only a confirmation, but a warning. He swore out loud as he climbed back on the Ovaro.

He rode north as the day neared its end, and finally spotted the Flint Hills rising up before him. A wide pathway in the low hills beckoned to him, and the wheel marks told him Solita had led the others in this way. The hills quickly grew more rugged, the trail narrowing, widening and narrowing again. He saw the two wagons first, pulled over against a hillside. The path in front of them had turned into a passage only wide enough for two horses abreast. "She went on," Harry called out to him and Fargo steered the pinto into the narrow passage.

He'd ridden perhaps another ten minutes when the passage suddenly ended, widening into a massive formation of jumbled rocks piled high atop one another in careless profusion. A line of hills dotted with caves spread out behind the rocks, the huge pile of rocks blocking off most of their entrances. Solita stood in front of the rock pile, a sheaf of paper in her hands, and Fargo recognized the withered Aztec parchments. She turned to him as he dismounted, her patrician facade clearly agitated, clouded in bitter disappointment. "All for nothing. All for nothing," she bit out.

"What do you mean?" Fargo queried.

"This is the place," Solita said, waving the pieces of parchment frantically at him. "The maps, the conquistador notes, the Aztec writings, they all point to this place. This is where Coronado gave up and turned back empty-handed. This is where the Aztec warriors buried the sacred objects. This is where the chase ended. But nothing's here."

"You can't be sure about that," Fargo said.

"Everything I have agrees—the Aztec writings, the Spanish notes, all the maps. Only this can't be the place." She pointed to glyphs and drawings on the Aztec parchments. "They all described these landmarks; a huge, old red cedar, a cave right behind here with a line of hawthorns in front of it, a place where the ground rises up in a kind of platform. But none of these landmarks they wrote about are here. This collection of big rock slabs are not even mentioned. This is the wrong place. After all this, it's the wrong place." Fargo took one of the maps from her. "I can't understand it. I just can't," she said in disgust.

There was still daylight left, so Fargo walked slowly, her map in hand, bent low, crawling through tight spaces, making his way through the big rock slabs that jutted upon and against each other. He walked outside the jumble of rocks, circling the entire area, his eyes scanning every foot of ground, pausing to measure with his eyes, bending over to follow marks imbedded deep in the soil, peering at scrapings on flat stones. Finally he halted his wandering and returned to Solita. An ordinary woman would have been reduced to tears of disappointment and frustration at what she'd found, he was certain. But not Solita. There was anger and spite in the tight lines of her lovely visage, but she still kept her emotions in check behind that regality she could so easily wear.

He wondered if she ever let her emotions loose as he paused before her.

"Maybe not," he said simply and quietly as dark deepened.

She frowned at him. "Maybe not what?"

"Maybe this isn't the wrong place," he said and her lush, lovely lips fell open. It took her a moment to pull them closed.

"But where are the landmarks? Nothing's here that's supposed to be here. It's all changed," she said, her sentences practically gasps.

"That big red cedar was here. I saw what's left of the base of it. Root marks stay a long, long time," he said and she stared at him, unable to comprehend his words.

"I . . . I don't understand," she murmured, finally.

"Seems to me you've forgotten the pyramids of Cholula. Cholula was in what is now the modern province of Pueblo, Mexico," Fargo said.

Her stare grew wider. "How do you know about that?" she questioned.

"Learned the story of it once when I was in Chihuahua," he said.

"How does it fit here? I don't understand," Solita said.

"Tell me about the pyramids of Cholula," he said.

"They were sacred Aztec places when the people heard that the Spanish were coming. They knew the Spanish would steal whatever they could and desecrate the holy pyramids," she said and paused, saw his eyes holding on her.

"Go on," he said.

"They gathered every man, woman, and child, and put everyone to work and brought soil, bushes, trees, and plants. They covered the sacred pyramids from top to bottom. When the Spanish finally arrived in Cholula, they saw only small mountains of earth and trees and went on their way. The pyramids were saved for a long time. Only many years later did the Spaniards discover the pyramids buried under the disguise of the mountains the people of Chulula had made."

"Same thing here, I'm thinking," Fargo said. "Only Mother Nature did the burying."

"I still don't understand." Solita frowned.

"An earthquake hit this area after Coronado left and the Aztecs hid their sacred objects. It changed the face of everything here. It destroyed some of the hills and created new ones. It made these big slabs of jumbled stone. You can't see it anymore than the Spaniards could see anything but the mountains the people had made."

"The pyramids of Cholula," Solita breathed in awe.

"Disguises, made by people or nature. Your writings and maps aren't wrong. You're at the same place, only it's changed, made different," Fargo said.

"Aztec notes say the warriors buried the sacred objects in a cave here," Solita said. "It could still be here, buried behind all these rocks! Could you find it?" She came to him, her eyes glowing with the dark fire of excitement. "It'll be worth your while, I promise," she murmured.

"I don't know if I could find it," Fargo said. "But I

233

do know one thing. I'm not going to try until I get the truth from you, about everything." He saw the surprise leap in her eyes, and he watched it shake her self-control. "You level with me or I'm walking out now. Time's run out, princess. No more games," he said.

"Why'd you call me princess?" Solita asked sharply.

"Seemed right," Fargo said. "Now, do I get the truth?"

"Build a fire. I'll be back when the others are asleep," she said. He nodded as she took her horse, leaving the packhorse behind. Night fell as she rode through the narrow passage, and Fargo used the moonlight to find firewood. It wasn't long before a yellow firelight illuminated the flat space in front of the rocks. He lounged against a smooth slab of stone and found himself wondering if Solita would indeed level with him. Taking orders, obeying commands, none of that sat well with her. She'd even bristled when he called her princess. He'd not settle for less than the truth, all of it, he promised himself, as he wondered what that truth might be.

He dozed as the fire gained strength, waking when he heard the sound of the single horse walking through the passage.

13

Solita emerged from the passage, her long, willowy body swinging gracefully from the horse. Fargo's eyes widened. She walked slowly toward him clothed in a garment of diaphanous green silk, her raven black hair hanging loose. Halting in front of him, he saw her haughty demeanor take on a new sensuous dimension.

"You called me princess. You were more right than you knew, Fargo," she said. "I am indeed a princess of the ancient Aztec people. My blood goes back to the reign of the Aztec rulers. Do I surprise you?"

"Yes. And in another way, no," he said.

"My great, great, great, great-grandmother danced for those Aztec warriors before they fled the conquistadores. They say it was her powers that helped them elude Coronado, and I have inherited her powers. She, too, was called Solita ... Princess of the Aztecs, The Golden One. With her dance, she gave her powers. I will dance for you to help you as she did the ancient Aztec warriors. I know you do not believe in such things, but that does not matter. What only matters is that I believe."

She then lifted her arms, pulled the garment from her, and stood gloriously naked before him. Fargo's breath drew in sharply at the sheer beauty of her, a statuesque flawless loveliness that might have been carved by a great sculptor. The firelight turned her body into shimmering gold as it played and danced over the gold-flecked tones of her skin. He had only seen the effect caught in an occasional flash of sun. Now, it was as if she were painted in gold as the firelight curled around her.

"The Golden One," he heard himself breathe in awe. Flesh and blood carried down through the ages. The genes followed from body to body. That was an accepted truth. Maybe other characteristics did, too, he found himself wondering. But profound thoughts fell away before the absolute beauty of her as he watched the willowy shape of her long, slim waist and narrow hips. Long, gorgeously curved legs glistened in the firelight. Below her narrow waist, her little belly curved graciously down to the absolute sensuousness of her legs. Above her waist, a long rib cage rose upward and his eyes lingered on pert, heavy breasts that made a perfect union with her body. They began with a slow, shallow breathtaking curve that filled out in full pear-shaped cups.

Tiny, hardly protruding nipples of golden pink were set on equally small pink areolas. Lastly, his eyes held on the striking V that crowned her pubic mound, as black and dense as the jet-black hair that fell to her shoulders. Wild and dense, it curled its unruly way in every direction, reached out to touch the inside of her smooth thighs, a striking and unexpected contrast to the shining smoothness that was the rest of her. She took a step backward, her voice suddenly low, throbbing as he'd never heard it before.

"She danced to the music of conch shells, bells, pipes, and drums. I will dance to the music of my heart," she said. Spinning, she began to sway, her hips lilting from side to side, then her legs began moving, her body undulating in half circles. Her body found its own rhythm as she swayed and turned. She began to dance faster, executing pirouettes, tight twists, spinning gracefully to dance with a combination of ballet movements and belly-dance shimmies that was both sinuous and sexual. Her dancing grew still faster and the firelight turned her gold-flecked skin into a shining, shimmering gown. Her long, black hair whirled and flew as she spun, her dance growing still more frenzied.

Faster and faster she whirled, and her breasts stood out in a sensuous twirl of their own. She moved closer to him and thrust her hips forward, the dense, unruly nap echoing the wild abandon of her dance as it seemed to leap forward, a beckoning, taunting bush. As if possessed by something beyond herself, Solita danced as he'd never seen anyone dance, bending to the ground in serpentlike motions, flying into the air as a butterfly takes wing, rubbing her hands along her golden body as she writhed. She filled the night with sensual excitement and Fargo felt his body growing tight and hot, responding to the power of her dance.

Then suddenly, with a final, leaping twist in midair, she came down in front of him, lying with her legs stretched sideways, her breasts heaving beautifully as she drew in deep breaths. She said nothing for a long minute, her ebony eyes fastened on him. "Beautiful," he gasped. "Truly beautiful."

Finally she spoke, her voice still throbbing and low. "The dance is not complete. Its powers are not fully realized." She reached out and clasped her arms around his neck. She needed no more words. He pulled off his clothes as the slightly musky odor of her assaulted him with an overpowering sexuality. He touched her skin, a faint coating of perspiration adding to its silky smoothness. She turned, and brought one beautiful breast up to his lips. He sucked it into his mouth, his tongue tracing a path around the tiny, pink-gold tip. "Aaaaah, ah, yes," Solita murmured and pushed herself deeper into his mouth, slowly turning, letting skin savor skin, letting tastes and tongue combine.

Her hands fluttered up and down his body. "Nice, oh, nice . . . good, good," she said, drawing her breast away and bringing her lips to his in a wet, hungry kiss. Her tongue danced in his mouth just as fervently as her body had danced minutes before. With a groan, she finally pulled away and his hands caressed her full, pear-shaped globes, moving down across the slightly damp smoothness of her. She turned and groaned as he caressed her smooth, heaving belly. Her

238

voice deepened, becoming a guttural cry of pleasure as he found the unruly, dense triangle. He pressed into the soft mound as the gossamer strands curled around his fingers, each a small tendril urging his hand to stay.

He let his hand slide downward, still resting against the warm moistness on her thighs, her eternal flower of passion. Solita's voice became a low, pulsing moan. He slid down further, found her portal of creamy softness and her throbbing sound became a deep cry that echoed against the stones. He pressed, slowly exploring her, and her cry turned into a scream. "Ah, ah, aaaaaah, oh, yes!" she breathed and her thighs slapped against him and then fell open. She thrust herself upward, turning and twisting, her flesh imploring, making its own demands. Her hands reached out and found his shaft and she gave a feline growl. She pulled him toward her, thrust herself upward again as he entered her sweet dark tunnel, feeling the warm nectar of her, the welcome of all welcomes.

Her legs drew up, resting high against his hips as she maneuvered to take all of him inside of her, sliding herself back and forth on him. He suddenly realized she was dancing again for him. She moved with the rhythm of passion, drawing upon every sense, begging of every sensation, and her moans filled the night. She clung to him, arms and legs wrapped around him. She gripped him harder, her patrician composure shattered on the altar of uncontrolled pleasure. His own passions were about to burst forth when Solita's moans suddenly became sharp screams. He felt her breast quiver in his mouth, against his face, her body tighten around him, her cream-soft inner walls contract to seize him tightly.

Her scream rose to an ear-piercing shriek, renting the night as she thrust herself upward. She found words in between her screams. "Now, now, now, yes, oh Gods of Gods, yes, yes, yes!" He exploded with her and they became one, flesh trying to delay the inevitable, the body clinging with its every sense, enjoying, crying out in its own way, savoring every fleeting moment of feeling, touching, tasting. But finally she lay against him, sweet mewlings still coming from her lips, her smooth skin made smoother by the faint coating of sweat that still lingered from her dance. But the dance that followed the first one, the frenzied coupling dance, hadn't really ended yet. It had become a slow waltz of bodies still locked together, of little murmurings that finally ended.

She lay beside him and he took in her beauty, still in awe of her breathtaking loveliness. The firelight had burned low, but still her skin glowed with flickers of gold. He lay with her quietly until she turned and rose up on one elbow, one lovely breast dipping to press against his chest. "You'll search in the morning and you will have powers you never had before," she said. "You will see as you never have before, know as you have never known before."

"I never turn down help," Fargo said. "But you've a lot more to tell me. Telling me you're an Aztec princess isn't enough. I want to know why you're going through all the motions for a phony expedition."

"Why do you say it's phony?" She frowned.

"Because you don't give a damn about the things you've had everyone doing. You don't care about tracing the plants, trees, birds, and animals. You didn't think twice about abandoning the artifacts that were dug up. Why?" he pressed. "Why the act?"

"Self-protection. Nobody bothers a scientific expedition," she said.

"Somebody did. All those attacks, all those attempts to stop you," he pressed.

"I told you, they all expected I'd be carrying a lot of money. That's what they were after," Solita said.

"I didn't buy that then. I don't now," Fargo said, considered a thought for a moment, and decided it was past time for games. "Who's Santos Arriaga and why'd he back you?" he asked.

Solita's face flooded with astonishment. "How'd you learn that?"

"I've ways," he said.

"What ways?" she demanded, sitting up, her heavy breasts swaying as she did.

"That's not important. Tell me about Arriaga," he said as he realized how hard it was to concentrate while arguing with a beautiful naked woman.

"I needed money to put the expedition together. It takes money to buy wagons, hire diggers and guards, and hire the best trailsman in the country," she said. "I made him a proposition and he agreed."

"Fifty percent of what?" he asked.

"Dammit, you know too much. You went through my things. Somehow, someway. That has to be it," Solita said angrily.

He ignored her. "Fifty percent of what you find on the expedition, right?" he said.

"That's right," she agreed a little too quickly.

"But I know you don't give a damn about what you find. What are you really looking for?" he pressed.

"The sacred objects. That's all I really care about, I'll admit," she said. "I want to return them to the descendants of the Aztec people. They are still a major part of our heritage. Everyone of royal blood has the duty to find the sacred objects. That's what I want."

His lips pursed as he peered at her. She sounded convincing. But not convincing enough, he decided. Too many things still didn't fit right. "Santos Arriaga doesn't sound like a man who'd spend a lot of money for fifty percent of some artifacts or antique objects, no matter how sacred to somebody else." She didn't answer and his eyes narrowed at her. "If I don't get the truth, I won't search," he said. "No more games."

She took a moment before she answered, a touch of sullenness in her voice. "Ancient Aztec writings list each of the sacred objects carried away to stop Coronado from getting them," she began. "They are worth a fortune. Most are solid gold. Many are decorated with precious stones—jade, emeralds, diamonds, rubies. Others are made of pure silver."

"What are you calling a fortune?" Fargo asked.

"I'd guess over a million dollars," she said.

He let a low whistle escape his lips. "That'll do," he

said. "No wonder Santos Arriaga was interested." He fastened a long stare at Solita. "But your only interest is in returning the other half to the descendants of the Aztec people," he said. She nodded but he caught a moment's uneasiness in her nod. "Why do I suddenly think Arriaga's not the only one interested in a million dollars?" Fargo pushed at her. Though beautifully naked, she somehow managed to return a glare of patrician superiority. But she didn't answer his question, he noted. "I'm right, dammit," Fargo threw at her. "You don't really give a damn about their being sacred objects." She continued to stay silent. "You don't want to return sacred objects. You want to sell them, just like Arriaga," Fargo said.

"Not just like Arriaga," she protested.

"Not much damned difference, either," Fargo said. "How do you think your ancestors would feel about that, princess?"

"I've thought hard about that. They'll be letting me know," she said soberly.

"A message from three hundred years ago?" he asked.

"Yes," she said firmly.

"How?"

"If we find them, it will be a sign they approve of what I'm doing. It will be like they're giving me permission," she said.

"And if we don't find them?"

"It'll be a sign they don't approve," she said. "So you see, it's not just up to me."

He turned her answer over in his mind, gave voice

to the thoughts that pushed at him. "You're a package of contradictions, princess," he said. "Part of you is in this world, part of you in another world ages ago. Part of you believes in experience and practical knowledge, part of you believes in strange powers and mysterious forces."

She smiled and wrapped her arms around him. "Right now, all of me believes in making love to you again," she murmured.

"We can arrange that," he said and she brought one breast to his lips at once. He pressed down upon her and it was but a matter of seconds before she made the night ring with her cries and moans. When the night grew still, he slept with her against him until the new day came. She woke with him, then pulled on the diaphanous green garment as he finished dressing. "Wait with the others. I search best on my own, without distractions," he said.

"If you find the cave, come get me. I want to go in with you," she said.

"All right," he said and it was only minutes after she left that the earth rumbled again. His eyes looked upward, then swept the rocks as the rumbling grew louder, then faded away, leaving only the sound of the hiss of boiling steam from new fissures. There had been no shaking, no quaking, no new cracks in the earth. But Fargo took little confidence in that. The rumbling had been more than an ominous sign. It had been a portent, a harbinger of things to come, he reminded as he himself strode to the tall jumbled pile of rocks.

He bent low to crawl beneath a narrow length of granite, letting his eyes trace the stone to where it lay across another rock. When he reached the corner he saw marks that told him where the granite had fallen atop the other rock. Drawing the Arkansas toothpick from its calf holster, he made marks at the spot in the rock which would be easy for him to follow. Following the second length of stone, he came to a square block that butted up against a rounded piece of sandstone. He used his knife to mark both pieces and saw a trail of pulverized stone that led him to a long section of eroded escarpments, with a narrow passage in between. Once again, deep ridges in the stone caught his eye but he made his own knife-scratch marks before moving through the narrow passage. When he emerged from the passage, he found himself facing a hill with a cave fronted by a growth of heavy brush and misshapen hawthorns.

He peered at the end of the escarpment and it became clear that it had never touched the cave in the hill beyond, but instead curved west toward another hill. Fargo followed it, seeing a line of low rocks that butted one another as though they'd been pebbles tossed there by a giant hand. He etched knife marks on each one as they led to the second hill, where he saw the mouth of another cave. This cave entrance had two large boulders in front of it that partially hid the entranceway. The two large stones had no connection with any other rock formations, he saw. They had plainly been put there by a quake that had sent them crashing down the hill.

Again, Fargo put knife marks on the stones and as he stepped back, he felt excitement spiral through him. Was this the cave? Was this where the fleeing Aztecs had finally eluded Francisco Vasquez de Coronado over three hundred years ago? Did a fortune in sacred objects lay hidden inside that cave?

Fargo forced himself to turn away and retrace his steps. He'd promised Solita he'd notify her as soon as he found anything promising. Besides, it was her show. She deserved being in on the victory. Or the defeat. As he followed the scratch marks he had made on the rocks, one fact kept prodding at him. He had found the marks and indentations that had brought him here with an ease that surprised him. It was just luck, he told himself, but something inside him refused to let him believe it.

He managed an oath of irritation just as another rumble broke into his thoughts, longer and louder this time. The tremor shook the rocks around him, and suddenly Fargo saw a piece of rock break away and crash to the ground. He reined to a halt and felt another faint quiver. A large quiver soon followed, and he immediately put the Ovaro into a canter. He found Solita waiting for him astride her horse, the packhorse behind her. "Did you find the cave?" she asked at once.

"I think so, but we can't go in, not now," he said.

"Of course we can," she said. "Come on."

"There's a quake coming, and damn soon. We'll never get out alive if we're caught in there," he said.

"And if it comes, we might never get in there.

Everything could be destroyed. I'm not waiting for that," she said, and swung from the horse and ran to the packhorse, pulling out two short-handled shovels. "Show me where the cave is, dammit," she said and started to run along the rocks.

He swore as he ran after her, pointing out the way by using the marks he'd scratched. He felt another strong tremor as they reached the cave, but Solita skirted the two big rocks and plunged right through the entrance. Fargo followed, and halted beside her where a series of small mounds of earth rose up not far from the mouth of the cave, seemingly part of the cave wall. Some were covered by moss a foot thick, others by a blanket of small stones. "There, under those mounds! I know it. I feel it," she breathed and, using one of the little shovels, she began to attack the first lichen-covered mound.

He took the other shovel and began to dig into the next mound. They were shoveling furiously when the cave trembled. "Let's get out of here," Fargo said.

"No," she flung back as she continued to dig. Fargo cursed and kept digging with her. He reached the bottom of his mound first, and saw a piece of cloth wrapped around something. Pulling it free, he unwound the cloth and held up a chalicelike cup of solid gold that glittered even in the dim light. He heard Solita gasp in awe, and turned to see her holding a long sceptre of gold encrusted with rubies and emeralds. He saw another cloth at the back of his mound and brought it out to find a wandlike object fashioned of silver with gold trim. Solita uncovered another drinking vessel, this one of gold, rimmed with sparkling diamonds.

They attacked the next mound together, then the next, as the cave continued to tremble. When they had finished, Fargo stared at an array of gold, silver, and gem-encrusted objects ranging from chalices, to urns, to special Aztec religious pieces, to priestly necklaces and amulets. Fargo was certain Solita's estimate of their value was not exaggerated. "We'll load all we can on the packhorse, and carry the rest out ourselves," she said. "Let's get started."

"Guess again, honey," a voice suddenly said. Fargo spun to see Clea. Harry stood beside her, pointing an army carbine at them.

"What are you doing here?" Solita asked, glaring in surprised fury.

"We're here to get very rich," Clea said and walked over to the array of objects, adding a new air of propriety to her usual tomboy swagger. Fargo saw her toss him a smile as she passed. Solita's eyes fixed on Clea in an unbelieving stare.

"Waiting does pay off." Harry chuckled as Fargo's eyes flicked to the carbine. Harry caught his glance. "Don't even think about it, cousin. I don't want killing, but I sure as hell will if I have to," the man said. Harry Paxton wasn't the kind to bluff, Fargo was certain.

"You've been waiting since the very beginning, haven't you? This was no last-minute thought," Fargo said.

"Ever since we met Vittorio," Clea put in.

"The cook who died," Fargo said.

"He had the fever for weeks before he kicked in," Harry said. "He talked a lot. Told us all about the expedition and what Solita figured to find. Told us about Santos Arriaga, too."

"Arriaga had arranged it so that Solita would hire Vittorio as a cook," Clea said with a derisive laugh directed at Solita. "Arriaga wanted Vittorio on the expedition so he could report back to him. He was sure you never intended to split with him. He told Vittorio you'd take it all for yourself."

Fargo glanced at Solita. Her face had become twisted in icy rage. "Was he right?" Fargo asked.

"Stay out of this," she hissed.

"I'll be damned," Fargo said. "You going to stiff your ancestors, too?"

"I said stay out of it," Solita growled, her eyes locked on Clea. Fargo turned to Harry and Clea.

"Arriaga was behind trying to lynch you two. He didn't want you two in as cooks. He wanted time to plant somebody else for himself," Fargo said.

"Bull's-eye," Harry said. "Lucky for us, you happened by." Harry's laugh had a lot of things in it. Gratitude wasn't one of them.

"Enough talk. I'll start carrying things out of here," Clea said. She began to gather up some of the smaller items when Solita's scream split the air.

"No!" she shrieked, the sound a mixture of defiance and outrage. Fargo saw her long figure hurl itself through the air, barreling into Clea, who had her arms full of objects. "Bitch! Rotten little slut!" Solita cried out as Clea went down, valuables spilling out of her arms. Fargo started for the two girls but Harry raised his carbine.

"Stay back," he said and Fargo returned his eyes to Solita. She had seized Clea's short hair, pulling mightily on it. Clea howled but Solita lost her grip and Clea rolled away. But Solita still maintained the advantage and her long arms lashed out, raking across Clea's face, then encircled Clea's throat, throwing the smaller girl to the ground. Battling with total blind rage, Solita tried to bring her foot down on Clea's back as the smaller woman rolled. She missed but followed with a diving leap, landing atop her opponent. "You'll not get your hands on any of this, you thieving little whore!" Solita rasped, curling one arm around Clea's throat.

Though Solita had the advantage of surprise, raging anger, a body of lean strength and dancers' muscles, Fargo saw the aggressive tomboy in Clea surface. Using her leg, Clea brought her knee up and kicked backward. The blow caught Solita low, smashing into her pelvis. Solita gasped in pain and lost her grip as she fell back. Clea spun at once, kicked out again, this time catching Solita in the stomach and her lithe figure doubled up as if she were a piece of straw. Solita tried to recover but was still gasping for breath as Clea went at her, smashing a solid punch into her jaw. Solita fell to her side and Clea kicked at her again, but Solita managed to reach out and wrap her hands around Clea's calf. She pulled hard and Clea went down with a cry of pain.

Solita whirled, and came at her, having to dodge back as Clea kicked and punched as she rolled on the ground, not unlike a spinning top. "Stop them, dammit!" Fargo said to Harry.

"Five dollars on Clea," Harry chortled. Fargo started forward again but Harry swung the carbine at him as Solita and Clea fought on the ground. But other forces suddenly intervened with the terrible suddenness that Fargo had warned about. No minor trembling this time, the very earth split open. The ceiling of the cave began to come down in a shower of dirt and boulders. Fargo spun, seeing Harry go down under the first deluge of dirt. The man was almost instantly buried up to his waist as more earth and debris rained down on him. Fargo's eyes cut to Solita and Clea. They had stopped fighting, but both were scrambling to gather some of the precious objects even as a barrage of soil and rocks cascaded down on everything.

Fargo stepped toward Harry, who was now buried up to his armpits. A hail of rocks fell as the cave shook even more violently, and Fargo halted as he saw Harry Paxton's skull split open before the man disappeared under the deluge of falling earth. Fargo ran toward Solita and Clea. They were still trying to pick up things to carry out. He felt another violent quake, and looked up to see a large piece of rock hurtling down in an avalanche of earth. He hurled himself forward, his arms outspread, and smashed into Solita and Clea, grabbing both around their waists as he flung them forward. He felt a huge boulder crash into the ground where they had been a split second before, sending its own shock waves across the cave floor.

He looked back and saw Solita and Clea follow his gaze. Bits and pieces of gold, silver, and gems arced into the air as the boulder smashed everything into bits. "No, no, no!" he heard Solita cry hysterically. She pushed to her feet, her dark eyes blazing with anger, disappointment, and unfulfilled obsession. Clea rose beside her and Fargo saw furious greed alighting on her round face. Both started for whatever precious objects were left beyond where the boulder had landed. They began to run through the rain of dirt that still descended heavily from the roof of the cave.

Fargo grabbed hold of both as they tried to move by him, spinning them around and slapping each across the cheek. They halted, blinking in surprise, their frenzy abated. "You're not going to be rich, damn you! You're going to be dead, like Harry," he said to Clea, his eyes boring into Solita. "You wanted a sign. You got it. Your ancestors don't approve and I don't blame them," he said. Solita stared back at him, her mouth open and her face torn and streaked with dirt. She still managed to look beautiful, Fargo marveled. He took both by their arms and flung them forward. "Run, dammit, run!" he yelled as he saw another giant piece of the cave collapse.

He stayed behind them as they reached the mouth of the cave. The two huge boulders that almost obscured the cave entrance remained but they had shifted, leaving more room beyond. As they stumbled out of the cave, Fargo came to a halt as he saw six figures standing there. One, a big, burly man with a black mustache and a Stetson decorated with Mexican silver, glanced at him and then at Solita. "We rode hard but it seems we didn't make it in time," he said to Solita.

"Santos Arriaga?" Fargo broke in as Solita stared at the man with odious contempt.

Arriaga nodded, then stepped forward and abruptly slapped Solita across the face. She didn't flinch, she just glared with pure hatred at Arriaga. Arriaga turned to Fargo. "I don't like being played for a fool. I'd like to salvage something out of this fiasco. Shooting all three of you will have to do," he said.

Fargo's eyes flicked across the altered landscape. Trees were uprooted, boulders had shifted to new places, hills had formed of newly moved upheavals of dirt. The quake had ceased but Fargo felt the faint trembling aftershocks of earth under his feet. It finally ceased, but not for long. His eyes cut to Arriaga. "I don't much like being shot. There's a lot of stuff still in one piece inside," Fargo said to Arriaga. "I'll show you where it is for a piece of it."

Santos Arriaga's smile was one of pure avarice. "You're an empty-headed fool. I've six men with me—we'll find it ourselves. But my thanks for the information," he said and gestured to one of the six men. "Stay and watch them. Shoot the first one that moves." Motioning to the others, Arriaga led them around the boulders and into the cave. They'd be a while searching, Fargo realized. He just had to be ready by the time Arriaga came out, raging at having lost the treasure to the quake. He glanced at the re-

253

maining man's holster, seeing that it held an old Remington five-shot double-action piece. The only advantage the man had was that his hand was already resting on the butt of the revolver. Yet Fargo knew he had outdrawn others who had that same advantage in the past.

He shifted his feet and prepared to act when suddenly he felt another tremor that soon became another quake. The earth rose in a tremendous eruption, and Fargo saw wide cracks open up and the hills begin to collapse. Solita, Clea, and Arriaga's man were thrown to the ground, as was Fargo, who managed to stay on one knee. He saw Arriaga's man shake himself, push halfway up from a prone position, and reach for his gun. "Don't even try it," Fargo warned. "Drop your hand."

"*Bastardo.*" The man snarled and yanked at his gun. Fargo's hand was a blur as he drew the Colt. The gun barked before the guard had the Remington leveled. The man shuddered and fell back. Fargo rose unsteadily as the earthquake continued. He looked back at the cave. A pall of smoke and dirt spewed from the mouth of the cave. The hill over the cave was hardly there anymore. It had collapsed in on itself and the cave below. He saw Solita and Clea staring, their faces wreathed in a mixture of emotions. Perhaps shock and disappointment were foremost, he decided. They then turned their eyes toward him.

"I expected you might be grateful, first," he said. Neither of them answered as they glanced once more to the cave. "Arriaga won't be coming out. None of them will," Fargo said. "I'm going back. It's over. You can come if you've a mind to." He left them there, walking back to where the Ovaro waited. Fargo had just swung into the saddle when Solita and Clea appeared together. He fixed a skeptical eye on them. "You going to go back together?" he asked.

"No. Why would you think that?" Solita frowned. "We've nothing in common."

"I wouldn't say that," Fargo remarked.

"What?" Clea asked.

"How about greed," he said. "Lying. Bending principles to suit yourselves." They just glared back at him, then got their horses and rode in silence along with Fargo as he returned to where Matt Benton and the remaining crew were waiting. There had been damage to the ground here, too, Fargo saw, but not as much as at the area around the caves.

Clea tethered her horse to the chuck wagon. "I'll be driving back with Matt and the others. We'll have plenty of food," she said. "You're welcome, of course."

"I'll be going my own way," Fargo said. "Been told enough tales, heard enough lies." He nodded at the others and turned the Ovaro. Solita was looking down at the saddle horn. She didn't look up as he paused beside her. "You're still beautiful, golden one. At least you've still got that left," he said and put the pinto into a trot. He headed into the Kansas plains, and started to circle around Wichita. Most of the land had been untouched by the quake, he noted, and the day was drawing to a close when he halted under a cluster of black willow near a pond.

He was setting out his bedroll when he saw the lone rider approaching slowly, pausing to peer down at his hoofprints. He waited until the rider came into view, and his lips pursed as Solita drew up beside the willows. She dismounted with her usual grace. She'd cleaned up, he noticed as she came to him. "I didn't just give you all lies," she said. "I wanted you to know that."

"Which one wasn't?" he grunted.

"I really am a princess, descended from the old Aztec people," she said.

"Fair enough" he said.

"My great, great, great, great-grandmother was the Golden One. She did dance for the warriors who kept the conquistadores from the sacred objects. She helped them win."

"Maybe she was a better dancer than you." Fargo smiled as he folded himself onto his bedroll. "You didn't win."

"Go to hell." Solita flared. He laughed and waited for her anger to subside. Once it did, she came to sit beside him. "Maybe I got too greedy, but I was going to bring back some of the sacred objects, and return them to those Aztecs still keeping the flame. It was maybe the only chance to do it. I'm glad at least that I tried."

"What do you mean the only chance?" Fargo asked.

"In just a hundred and forty years it'll be the beginning of a new century, the millennium. The Aztec calendar indicates they believed the world would end in the year two thousand. Or maybe just their part of it. It's not clear. But it would have been nice to return some things before that time comes around."

He thought for a moment. "Millenniums have come and gone before. Still, the world seems to go on," he said.

Solita's dark eyes suddenly held a mischievous light. "Maybe that other Solita was a better dancer. Maybe you're right, she could make things happen. But I bet I make love better," Solita said.

"There's no way you can prove that," he said with a smile.

"No, but I'm still sure of it," she said.

"Why?" he asked.

"I hope we've learned something in three hundred years," she said. "I'd like showing you again."

"That's the best idea you've had in a long time," Fargo said. She came to him, tearing her blouse off, offering all her lovely charms to him. There was a sweet hunger in the touch of her lips, the way she brought her beautifully shaped breast to his mouth. Maybe being greedy had its place, he reflected.